The Littlest Gun

The Littlest Gun

by

Paul L. Thompson

toExcel

San Jose   New York   Lincoln   Shanghai

The Littlest Gun

This edition published by toExcel Press, an imprint of iUniverse.com, Inc.

For information address:
iUniverse.com, Inc.
620 North 48th Street
Suite 201
Lincoln, NE 68504-3467
www.iuniverse.com

ISBN: 1-58348-320-9

Foreword

Janice McCord is fourteen years old when the five Kraymon brothers ride in and shoot down her parents and her twin brother Jack. She takes up Jack's name and her father's .45 to blaze a trail of revenge across the Territory of New Mexico. Outlaws are hot on her trail, but her fast shooting and sharp wit turns them from lawlessness to helping her track down the killers of her family. While in jail, arrested for the murders of her family, she writes her cousin, U.S. Marshal Shorty Thompson for help. Help does arrive, but she still joins the outlaw gang that killed her family. Now they are getting ready to pull off the largest robbery in the Territory's history. Over a million dollars will be crossing Tecolote Creek on Saturday. To make sure she is the one to get the killers of her family and the revenge she has sought for months, Janice may have to fight her three friends, and her cousin Shorty, along with half the U.S. Cavalry. She will do what she has to do, or get killed tying.

Chapter One

Alice McCord picked up her broom and walked out to sweep the porch. She loved the early mornings with birds singing and the smell of fresh air. As she pushed the dirt toward the edge of the porch, dust made a reddish gold hue in the sunlight. She was smiling, thinking of her family, when for some unknown reason, she stopped sweeping and lifted her eyes to the west.

She was unable hear the hoof beats yet, but could see five horsemen weaving their way down the road to the ranch. She muttered to herself, "why do men always run their horses so hard? Nothing is that important."

For the moment, Alice went back to her sweeping. Pounding hoof beats grew louder and louder. She called into the house for her fourteen year old son. "Jack, riders are coming, run to the barn for your dad."

Jack knew something was wrong by his mother's tone, and before he got to the front door, she had put her hands to her mouth to stifle the screams that were already exploding from her throat. "Oh my God! Dear Lord! Jack! Jack! Get back inside! Get your fathers' guns! Hurry, Jack!"

Jack jumped for the gun rack, just as his father heard his wife's screams, and came charging from the barn. Henry tried running between milling horses, and through dust so thick he could hardly see. He must make it to his wife, and the guns that could save their lives. He knew the Kraymon brothers.

Henry thought he was going to make it, until one of the riders fired his gun. Henry stopped dead still, in shock that he didn't feel the bullet slam into his body. Alice's screaming went to a high pitched keen as she ran to her son. Henry looked up to see Jack hanging half off the porch. He had been shot in the face. "If I had worn my guns this morning, this wouldn't be happening!"

Henry lunged forward, grabbing at the closest horseman to pull him to the ground, but was pistol-whipped to the side of the head. On hands and knees, and through dust and blood that covered his eyes, he saw two men grab his wife, and slam her to the porch, ripping the clothes from her body. Using a rope they tied her hands and spread her legs.

Henry felt the rope as one of the men dropped a loop around his neck. As the rope tightened, Henry's vision dimmed as though the dust had gotten thicker. He could no longer see, and the laughs of the men, and sounds of the horses were swiftly fading. Had Alice stopped screaming? Where is Janice? "Forgive me Lord, for not protecting my family." Everything went black.

A bucket of water in his face, brought Henry McCord from the dark depths of unconsciousness, to a world of reality. Alice was being raped and he was tied where he must watch. Alice was lying on her back, naked. Her eyes were closed, and her arms were tied above her head. Blood seeped from the corner of her mouth. The men had put a rope around each of her ankles, and spread her legs where she was fully exposed to their groping, probing, desires and wants. One of the men was busy humping her.

Sam Kraymon grabbed Henry by the hair and tilted his head where he had to watch, as the next man mounted Alice. "McCord, I told you I'd come lookin'! No man hits me in the face and gets away with it! Now you're gonna watch while me and my brothers take your woman. By the way, where's that pretty little daughter of yours? How old is she no way? Probably around twelve or fourteen, at least she's old enough to be broke in. Now would be a good time, I like 'em young. Where in the hell is she?" He hollered and laughed, badgering Henry by tugging at the rope, and choking him.

Henry glared at Sam, trying to remember where Janice might be. The first thing this morning she went to the river to plant blackberries, and hadn't returned. He closed his eyes, praying Janice wouldn't walk in on all of this. These men would use, and then kill her also. The grunts and groans of the man humping Alice, made him pray ever harder. "Lord, spare Janice!"

A sharp slap across the face made Henry open his eyes again.

"McCord, where in the hell's that daughter of yours? I'm gonna get some of that, if it's the last thing I do!"

Sam jerked Henry's hair again, laughing. "Stupid bastard! I'm going to kill all you McCords!"

Talking to his brothers, Sam wasn't in a hurry. "Ed, you hit that good stuff a time or two more, then get off. While Otis is pounding her, you and Nick and Jess search this place over for that sweet little daughter. Before this day is over, I'm going to throw the prod to her just like she was full growed. I'll bet she bucks and snorts beter'n her maw ever thought about doin'."

Alice lay still as each man helped himself to her body, and then took turns doing it again. She lost count of how many times each one did it. She was numb of all feeling, but wanted to reach and hold Henry's hand. He had given her love and a set of twins that were now fourteen years old. "But wait, Jack is dead! Oh, Janice, run! Run for your life! Run, and never look back!"

Otis was now between her thighs as she screamed and hollered at the top of her lungs. She was jerking and twisting with all her might. Otis rode her out, laughing. "Lady, if I know'd you was this wild, I'd wore my spurs!"

Henry was tied ten feet away to a porch rail, and could only watch his wife's pain. Again he thought of Janice. She is very good with a gun. Did she take one with her this morning? Would she try to use it against five men?

Henry McCord was watching as Sam Kraymon dropped his pants around his ankles and slid between Alice's trim, creamy smooth thighs. Henry tried getting loose, but the rope closed around his neck even tighter. He screamed at Sam. "Sam Kraymon, you're the lowest of dogs! Raping a helpless woman! You let me loose and give me a gun, and I'll kill every son-of-a-bitchin' one of you bastards! You and your whole damn bunch are rotten, dirty cowards!" Henry's eyes were closed, and Sam seemed to pay no mind to what was said. He was busy hunching and groaning. Sam, with his member still in Alice, pulled his gun and shot Henry between the eyes. Alice closed her eyes even tighter, shuddering at the sound of more gunfire. Leaving Alice's hands tied, Sam reached and cut the binds to her ankles. He smiled as he brought the gun barrel to the middle of her chest and pulled the trigger. He rode her through her death throes, then calmly withdrew himself from her body and pulled up his pants. "You was good, Lady. I gotta say that for you, damn good!"

"All right, let's get the hell out of here! That girl must have stayed in town over the weekend, and ain't home yet. We'll get her later. Nick! You listen here now, don't you go tellin' what we went an' done out here! I know you like little boys, but that woman was pretty damn good. I didn't mean to kill the boy until you got through with him. He just came running out the door with that gun, so I had to. Get that dumb assed look off your face! Let's ride!"

Nick half hung his head in disappointment, then brightly said, "Naw, Sam, the girl is here somewhere. When Otis was humping that woman, she kept screaming, Jane, Janice, or Jennifer or something like that."

Sam grabbed him by the front of his shirt, and flung him screaming to the ground. "Then don't stand here like a damn fool, get to lookin'!" They searched the house and both barns before giving up and riding off. After a few hundred yards Sam stopped his horse, and thought for a moment. "Hold up boys, you know, we might ought'a go back there and put them bodies in the house and burn it and them plumb down." Thinking better of it, he started riding off. "Naw, what the hell, nobody knows it was us what done it."

Chapter Two

It was a beautiful, quiet, sun filled morning. Janice was listening to songbirds, and planting blackberry bushes down by the river. She heard the screen door slam as someone came out on the porch. Moments later she heard her mother scream. Screams, screams so awful they were soul retching.

She could tell her mother was terrified. Something terrible was happening. Janice was frozen to the spot.

As she sat numbed with fear, gunshots were fired. Jumping to her feet, she ran toward the house. Fear ripped at her heart, making it want to explode from her small body. Why had she not brought one of her father's guns? Of all the days not to be ready for danger, why this one? She ran to the edge of the trees, and stopped, looking beyond the field. She watched in horror as five men brutalized and murdered her family. From her hiding place, Janice was blankly staring at the commotion and started screaming. She slapped her hand over her mouth, shouting, "My God, the Kraymon brothers! It's the Kraymon brothers! What are they looking for? Why don't they stop? Oh, please God, make them leave mamma alone!

"What are they looking for in the barns? Dear Lord! It's me, they're hunting for me! Help me God!" She turned and ran. Stumbling blindly, running down river, as limbs and snags ripped at her clothes and flesh. She had to find a safe place to hide. Her mind was a turmoil of raw fear. "They can't find me, I must survive so I can get revenge! And I will!" She was sobbing wildly. "I'll kill everyone of those low life snakes!"

Janice stayed by the riverbank overnight, terrified at the thought of having to return to the house. She curled herself into a ball at the base of a sandy bank, and tried falling asleep, but her mothers' screams kept ripping at her every thought. She would dose for a few moments, then sobs would vibrate her awake. She listened, only normal sounds of the night were heard. She lay awake for hours, then dropped into a sobbing sleep again.

With the morning light she sat with her face in her hands, uncontrollably crying. Before her on the ground lay her father, Henry J. McCord, her mother Alice, and her twin brother Jack. Yesterday morning, or was it the day before, she couldn't remember, but she had seen the Kraymon brothers slaughter them all. Janice knew what brought it all about.

Last Saturday the family had gone the twelve miles to town for their monthly supplies. As her mother stepped from the dry-goods store to the wooden walkway, Sam Kraymon had grabbed her around the waist, and kissed her full on the mouth. Her father had dropped a one hundred-pound sack of flour before planting a fist right in Sam's face, splitting his lips and busting his nose. Never had she seen her father so mad. Janice recalled her mother's very words.

"Those men are killers and will not let this pass!" Then in a quieter voice whispered, "I'm afraid for all of us."

Glancing over, Henry had looked at his wife's worried face, and patted her on the hand, saying, "If it'll make you feel any better, the next time we go to town, I'll wear my guns. Now let's not worry too much about the loud mouth Kraymons. Talk was all it was, just drunken talk."

Janice walked from one body to the next, as though one of them would start breathing and get up, saying everything was all right. She was in a daze, and wasn't seeing as she got a pan of soap and water to wash the splattered blood from her mother's face. Tears flooded down her cheeks as she mumbled. "It's all my fault this happened, Mamma! If only I had taken a gun with me this morning, this wouldn't have happened. Daddy always told me, 'Button' he would say, 'don't ever leave the house without a gun. You never know, you might run upon a rattler.' Well, Mamma, five snakes were here yesterday, and I had no gun to kill them with. Why, Mamma, why didn't I take one this morning?

"And just look at poor Jack, he should have gone with me, but he had to fix that latigo. Mamma, with Jack and daddy gone, who's going to break the colts? You know I can ride good, but nothing like Jack."

With tears streaming down her cheeks, she looked to the west. She needed help, but no one ever came this far. It was twelve miles to Analla, and forty-five to Lincoln, where there might be a doctor. She looked from her mother, to her father, and then to Jack. She didn't need a doctor, she needed an undertaker. Hysterically she screamed and sobbed. Shaking uncontrollably, she got up and stumbled blindly around the yard. First to the corrals, then into the barn, as though she were looking for help.

She stood and listened, the only thing she could hear was water rippling in the river. Not one songbird was singing. Even the ranch animals were unusually quiet. After several minutes, she let out a great sigh. "I've got to get hold of myself. Jack would have. He'd have taken care of everything." She continued cleaning up the bloody, gory mess. She moved the bodies, and with a shovel, spread dirt over the bloody ground. Using lye soap and hot water, she scrubbed the porch where her mother and Jack were killed. Then she started cleaning her father and Jack.

Janice took the longest time with Jack. Not only was he her twin, but he was also her very best friend. They had not been apart more than a few hours of the fourteen years of their lives. Now it would be a lifetime of separation. Sobbing, she screamed, "Oh, Jack, Jack, I'll miss you!"

It was almost dark before she lay a blanket over each still body, and turned to walk into the house. She had not eaten a thing since early morning, but was too nauseated to even think of food. From crying and sobbing so much, she had a headache, and was weak from dehydration. Going to her bedroom, she lay across the bed, sobbing. Bolting upright, she went to her folk's bedroom. "Now where did Daddy keep his other pistols? Maybe they're in the closet with the fifty caliber Sharps. Come morning I'd better find all of Daddy's guns and get them cleaned up and loaded. Those Kraymons might just come back to burn this place to the ground. If they do, I'll kill five of the lowest skunks this world ever saw, or I'll die trying!"

Janice was glad her father and Jack had taught her how to use a gun by the time she was ten years old. Now, at fourteen, she was better than Jack ever was, and knew how to handle both a pistol and rifle. Before, it was fun because Jack did it, but now it would be a necessity. To think about all this, scared the breath from her small body. "God, show me what to do, and how, so I can do what I must!"

Janice slept a restless, frightful night but was up by five and had her breakfast on. As bacon was frying, a slight breeze whipped at the curtain through the open window. She lifted her eyes to look at the top of the hills. Though the sun wasn't touching the river valley yet, the mountaintops were a bright gold, flooded with light. Tears welled in her eyes as she remembered having to bury her family this morning. "All the Kraymons will die, I swear! God, you will be my only witness to this, and I will kill them, all!"

After dabbling at her food, she went to the barn and harnessed a big black plow horse. With the horse hooked to the hay sled, she drove around to the front of the house. Half-lifting, and half-dragging, she loaded her parents and Jack on the foot high sled. Breathing heavily, and sweating profusely, she walked back to the barn and got a shovel and grubbing pick. Holding the reins, she walked along beside the sled as the horse pulled it to a beautiful spot between long rows of apple and peach trees. The whole family had worked mighty hard, putting in this orchard. Every tree was spaced just right. The riverbank had made a beautiful location for the orchard. The soil here would be easy to dig.

Before throwing the first shovel of dirt, she started crying so hard it scared the horse. "Whoa, you stupid horse! I'll shoot you!" The horse looked at her, out of big round, rolling eyes, while moving it's ears back and forth, and lifting a front leg.

Janice looked at the horse, then put her arms around its neck, and softly sobbed. "I'm sorry I hollered at you, Hotshot. Hotshot, what am I going to do? Everyone I love has been murdered! I'm all alone!" She started crying again.

It was just before noon when she finished digging the first grave. Tying a rope under her father's arms, and using the horse, she lowered him slowly into the ground. Reluctantly she threw in the dirt. When the mound was about a foot high, she started crying. Sobbing, she screamed, "Daddy, I love you! Oh God, please help me! Oh why, God, why did this happen to us Lord? Oh why, why did you let my family die?"

Before digging the other two graves, she felt stinging in her palms.

She had blisters as large as her thumb, and two had already burst. She was filthy, dirty, and her hair was wringing wet with sweat. She was getting so weak, she had to go to the house to eat. Walking toward the house, she stopped dead still. "Oh my God! I plumb forgot about milking the cows this morning!" She ran to the barn and let the calves in with their mothers. "That will take care of that. But God, I can't do it all. What am I going to do?"

It was seven o'clock that evening when she walked back into the house and lay down. Again she was just too tired to eat supper, but nibbled a bit, and her hands were stinging with pain. She got up and rubbed wool fat onto the sores and blisters.

"God do I ever need a bath! I can smell myself! Yech!"

Working in the barn from early morning until dark, it took her five days to make grave markers for all three graves. Half of that time was spent working, then crying and swearing to get the Kraymons. "In the morning I'll put these on the graves, then start hauling rocks to cover them good. And I'll even build a good, strong fence to keep the cows and horses off the graves. Jack would have. I know he would, he always thought of everything.

The markers were larger than most she had seen, but she wanted them to be very visible and easy to read. When finished, she stepped back, and read them aloud, then dropped to her knees, sobbing. "Henry J. McCord, age 36. Died May 14, 1878. Alice McCord, age 32. Died May 14, 1878. Janice McCord, age 14. Died May 14, 1878.

"God, to you and anyone else that might be listening, my heart is lying in those graves! Janice McCord will not live again until every one of those Kraymons are dead, and I mean stinking rotten dead, by my hand! This I swear on these three graves!"

Chapter Three

Janice turned hard the weeks following the burial of her family. She never smiled, and no longer talked to the animals. Never singing, only mumbling to herself. All the animals could tell the difference in her. She set herself a routine; breakfast at five o'clock; feed the animals at a quarter of six, then take her father's guns and fifty shells to the creek bank and practice firing until ten. Her shoulder and wrist hurt so bad, tears filled her eyes. She would hold her wrist under the cool, soothing water of the creek to relieve the swelling, it helped.

"Lord, you can make me sore as you want, but I'm not going to quit until I'm fast, and good enough with these guns, to beat, out draw, and kill the rotten Kraymons dead!"

Tomorrow she would go into town and buy supplies. On top of the list were shells for the .45s and the .44 rifles. It was time to turn from girl to boy.

That evening she bathed and cut her long blonde hair, crying with every snip of the scissors. Rummaging through Jack's things, she found several pairs of pants and shirts that had been too small for Jack for some time.

They were still too large, so she got out her mother's new treadle sewing machine. An hour later most people wouldn't be able to tell her from Jack. Maybe they wouldn't notice she was a bit smaller, or her hips that had started to round out a bit. As she pulled on the first pair of pants, she looked herself over in her mother's mirror. Then she slipped on the large shirt, perfect. Her bumps didn't show enough to tell, she hoped.

Janice took care of all her chores before hitching a gray horse to the buckboard and heading the twelve miles to town. This was her first trip... alone. She wasn't worried; she had her father's loaded guns at her side, and knew how to use them. The tree-lined road running along the Rio Hondo was a beautiful river ride this time of year. If her parents and Jack were along, they would be singing a song, or just laughing and talking. This trip, Janice rode in silence. A happy thought, then a tear of sadness filled every mile.

As she pulled into Analla, she wondered why it was even called a town, but it was growing, and the only one in the Rio Hondo Valley. Janice pulled the horse to a stop in front of the bank, which was three doors down from the sheriff's office.

Nervously she looked around. She had to remember she was Jack. As she stepped down from the buckboard, Mrs. Bennett walked by. "Good-morning, Jack. How are your folks? I haven't seen them in church, lately.

Haven't given up on the Lord, have they?"

"Oh, hello Mrs. Bennett. No, I'm sure not, and I'll be sure and let them know you asked about them. They've been pretty busy, getting ready for a long trip. They're going all the way to St. Louis, to get my grandpa." Telling a lie made her grimace, but she figured she had better get good at it, at least for a while. Maybe God would forgive her.

Janice walked into the bank and bumped into Sheriff Norval. "Howdy, Jack. Where's your dad? Hadn't seen him in quiet a spell."

"Howdy, Sheriff Norval. Dad and Mom are getting ready to take a trip, so they sent me into town for supplies."

"Well I'll say. A long trip, huh?" Where are they headed, and how long do they expect to be gone?" Norval wasn't nosy, he was just asking.

"They're going plumb to Saint Louis. Grandpa's moving out here to live with us. They're going back to help him on the trip. They'll be gone well over two months, maybe even three." Janice hated lying, but it was necessary.

"Bad time of year to be doing that, ain't it? With most all the planting still to be done. Won't have much of a crop by the time he gets back."

"Dad took real good care of that. He's got the Rogers boys handling all of that. I'll just have to open the water ditches now and again, unless it rains."

"Those are mighty fine boys. They'll do him a right good job. Well, you be careful, Jack. I'll see you the next time you're in town." Sheriff Norval started on out the door, but stopped and turned around. "Oh, by the way, Jack, y'all ain't had no trouble out that way, as of late, have you? Sam Kraymon told me something about hearing a lot of shooting going on out there this past month. Said a whole bunch of it."

"Naw, no trouble. We've just got us a pack of wolves making a run at several young calves. We've about got it handled though. Is Mr. Kraymon around today?" Was she fast and bold enough to confront Sam Kraymon, now? Her palms started sweating, and she may have stammered when she spoke.

Janice's heart was beating so fast, she swallowed hard to get her breath.

"Naw, Sam and them brothers of his went over towards Silver City for awhile. They're sure a bad lot. Whole darned county's safer without them here. Far's I'm concerned, them are some worthless men."

"Yes, Sir. You just don't know how worthless."

Janice walked over and took a chair, waiting for Mr. McFarland to finish with a customer. A couple of minutes later the banker called Jack through the little wooden gate.

"Hello, Jack my boy, how are you today?"

"Fine, Mr. McFarland."

"Jack, I couldn't help over hearing what you said to Sheriff Norval. Will Henry be needing some of his money for that long of a trip?"

"Yes, Sir. That's what he sent me into town for. Also to pick up some other supplies." Janice knew she was breaking out in a sweat.

"That's just fine, Jack. How much will he be needing?"

"Five hundred dollars. And he wanted to know how much that would leave him in the bank." She was getting weak with fright, and short of breath.

"You wait right here. It won't take but a short minute." McFarland headed for one of his vaults, mumbling to himself.

Janice sat with her hands folded in her lap, looking all prim and proper. Everything was going much better, and faster than she had thought it would. No problems, yet, except a dry throat and trying to get her voice to work right.

Mr. McFarland was smiling as he brought a hand full of money to his desk. "Here you are, my boy. We'll just count it one more time, then I'll put it in this bean sack for you. I've written your father's balance on a piece of paper, and I'll put it in the bag where you won't lose it."

Mr. McFarland counted the money again, then put it and the note in the bag, closing it tight. As he handed it to Janice, he asked, "My goodness Jack! How come you have those fingernails so dad-gummed long? And have you been hit in the mouth? Your lips look a bit swollen."

"Huh? Oh, Oh, yeah! My horse slung her head and got me good. And I'm going to cut my nails tonight! I just had a bet with mom and Janice. I won. Well, thank you, Mr. McFarland. I'd best be getting home, Pa's waiting."

Janice went to the mercantile and got her supplies, and plenty of ammunition. She paid the bill and loaded her supplies before going to the gunsmith's shop. Hesitating for a long moment, she dried her palms on her pant legs, then went inside.

"Howdy, Mr. Peters. Do you think you can take up this gun-belt of my dads? He gave it to me, but it's too large." She handed him the belt.

"Naw, Jack, that'd be a little hard to do. But I believe I have one that will just about fit you. I made it for that Arron boy, but they moved away before I got finished with it. You're about his build. Here, try it on for size."

Janice smiled as she slipped the gun-belt around her waist. It was perfect. She paid three dollars, and said thanks. As soon as she was out of town, she took one of the .45s and slipped it in and out of the holster.

She flipped the reins along the horse's back, and hit a long trot, talking to herself. "Boy, being Jack is a lot tougher than I thought it would be. And these stupid finger-nails almost got me caught. I'm just too stupid prissy is all there is to it! But I won't be, just wait. The Kraymons are in Silver City, good. At least they're still in the country, where I can find them."

With breakfast, and the chores out of the way, Janice saddled a horse and rode over to Jesse Rogers' place. He was a tall, skinny fellow with an Adams apple as big as a horse turd. Every time Janice saw him, she giggled.

"Mr. Rogers, we need some planting done, and wondered if Eldon and maybe Don could give me a hand. I sure need some help."

His Adams apple bobbed up and down, and then centered in his throat.

"I'll send over Don and Eldon by the end of the week."

"Thank you, Mr. Rogers. I know Dad will be thankful, too."

As Janice rode back home, she thought of how she had acted while talking with Mr. Rogers. "I spoke polite, but not sissified. I sat with my hands on the saddle horn, and even spit twice. Gosh dang it, I forgot to look him in the eyes! Dang it all, I've got to remember to do that when I'm talking with someone. Oh my goodness! I sat with my hands in my lap at the bank, in front of Mr. McFarland! I was a total idiot! I wonder if he noticed? I've got to stop that! I am Jack McCord! And when I walk, I've got to remember to waddle, and have at least one hand in a pocket."

Janice got back home and after putting the horse away, she walked down to the orchard. Standing in front of the graves, beads of sweat formed along her upper lip. Uncontrollably, she was scared. Chills ran down her spine as if the temperature had suddenly dropped fifty degrees.

"Oh, my God! I can't let Eldon and Don see these graves! Not yet!"

For the next two days, from sunup until dark, Janice hauled hay and covered the graves and markers. Inside the fence it would look as if the hay was being kept away from the cattle. It was a job well done.

Her routine couldn't change that much. She would still practice her shooting. Tomorrow would be Friday, that meant the Rogers boys would be here first thing to start plowing. Janice sat alone on the porch, wondering what she was going to do. She looked up at the moon, and tears filled her eyes. Damn, but she missed her family. She walked inside and got the sack of money that Mr. McFarland had given her. Stacking it into neat piles, she picked up the note with the bank balance written in big letters. One hundred and fifty- nine thousand dollars. "A hundred and fifty-nine thousand dollars! My God, I'm rich! I can hire all the men I'll need to track down and kill everyone of them Kraymons!" She sat still for a moment, shaking her head from side to side. Beating her small fist on the table, she stood up.

"No, no I can't do that! It wouldn't be right, I have to do it myself, Jack would have. When I kill 'em, I'm going to be looking them right in the eye. They've got to know its me, a McCord doing the killing! I'll get everyone of them, or they'll get me! And I think I'm better with a gun than they are."

Keeping some of the money out, and hiding the rest, she went to sleep thinking of how good she was getting with the .45s and the .44 rifle. The rifle had her shoulder bruised and her wrist hurt from the .45s, but she was getting faster, and much stronger. "I'm good, and fast, but I'm going to be the best. I've got to be. When I'm good enough, I'm going after them bas..., devils!"

It was really too late for planting, and if not for looks, Janice wouldn't have had it done. But, if the crops didn't mature, she could turn the cattle in on it for winter-feed. Over the next three weeks the planting went well, and the days were hot and dusty. The territory needed rain. If not for the irrigation ditches, and all of that river water, nothing would even get out of the ground.

Early every morning after the chores were done, Janice saddled her horse and rode off toward the east. A mile and a half below the house, the Rio Hondo had made a cut between two hills, and Janice rode to the far side of that, and practiced with her guns for three hours.

Eldon had one hand in a pocket as he stepped in front of Janice's horse. "Jack, why do you ride off to the east, every morning?"

She jerked the reins to keep the horse from stepping on him. "Oh, we've got a few head of cattle over that way, and I gotta keep an eye on them." Janice was very quickly getting mad.

"Every day?" He had one eye closed, and the other eyebrow raised.

"Yeah, there's some baby calves among them, and we don't want wolves doing a thinning job." Janice was getting pissed off at his questions.

"I thought most of y'alls cattle was west and south of here."

"Goes to show you what thinking to can do for a feller, huh, Eldon?"

Eldon looked up at her for a moment, then asked, "What do you mean, Jack?" Janice knew without a doubt, Eldon was a little thick between his ears.

"If you don't think, very seldom will you be wrong. We've got our largest herds out on the plains east of here." She rode off in a huff. "What business is it of his where I go, or when I go?"

The day before the planting was finished, Janice came riding back in from her practice. Two men were at the corrals unsaddling their worn-out horses. Don and Eldon were standing against the fence with their heads down. Janice rode up slow and easy, hesitating to dismount. "What's going on here? Who are you men?" The silence was strong. She could hear one of the horse's tails swap at flies. Another ground its teeth on a steel bit and stomped the ground, wanting water.

One of the men turned with his gun pointed at her face. His left hand whipped straight out, toward Don and Eldon, as though to hold them against the fence they were already leaning on. Maybe he thought they might try and interfere, but their guns were already in the dirt. "Just fixin' to barr'ie a couple of yore horses. And that'n yer on looks like a good'n to me. Get off feller, 'fore I blow you out'a that saddle!" Janice saw his black stubble teeth as he talked. The man was filthy, and reeked of wood smoke. Janice wasn't scared, she was boiling mad. The horse she was on was Jacks. Nobody was going to steal her! Nobody! This was the best looking blaze faced sorrel in the whole New Mexico Territory.

The leather of her saddle creaking was the only sound as she slowly dismounted, and moved back and to her right. As the man took the reins in his left hand, Janice's nose wrinkled at the stink of a filthy, sweaty, unwashed skunk. She held her breath as she took four steps backward, almost gagging. Holding his gun in his right hand, the man put his left boot in the stirrup. When he reached with his left hand for the saddle horn, his eyes flicked that way, and he started to swing into the saddle. Janice drew her gun and fired. The bullet caught him full in the chest. As he fell back, the other man let go of his horse's reins, and grabbed for his gun. Janice shot him in the face before he could clear leather. He was slammed back into the fence, and fell to the ground, kicking hard a few times before relaxing in death.

Eldon and Don stood for a long moment with their mouths open. A barn door hinge squeaked, as a breeze built for just a moment, then died away. Eldon finally found words to speak. "Dad-gum-it Jack! That's the best shooting I've ever seen. You got both of 'em! And that one already had his gun out! Boy are you ever fast with that .45!" The sound of the shots still echoed in his head. He was pale with fear, and wringing wet with sweat.

Don walked over and slapped Janice on the back, knocking her a couple of feet. "Sorry, Jack, I didn't mean to hit you so hard, but darn yer fast with that gun. I'd bet very few growed men could beat you, huh, Jack?"

Janice was sick at her stomach at seeing the men she had just killed.

Slowly she put her .45 back in its holster. Placing her hand over her mouth, she retched a couple of times, but didn't vomit. She was pale as a snow cloud.

Don and Eldon had picked up their guns and holstered them. Eldon looked at Janice. "What's wrong, Jack? You sick er something? You ain't gonna start puking, or anything like that, are you?"

"Darn-it all to heck, I ain't ever killed nobody before! Just them two!"

"Naw, but you sure done a whoop up job on them, so they wouldn't steal your horses. And who knows, they might not'a let us live, once it was done. Yeah, bet they'd killed us, huh?"

Janice was still in shock at what she had done, and had the taste of bile in her throat. Eldon looked up and pointed to the west. "Riders coming in fast! Hope it's not some of these fellers friends. We could be in a world of hurt. Me and Don had better slip into the barn where we can get the drop on them. You find out what they want. Jack! Dad-gum-it, snap out of it!"

The riders brought their sweating horses to a sliding halt about ten feet from Janice. She hadn't moved as the dust settled over her, and her knees started to buckle. Looking up she saw it was Sheriff Pat Garrett and a posse. Don and Eldon came walking out of the barn. Pat Garrett was the first to speak. "Don, Eldon, looks like you boys done right well. Killed both of these scoundrels before I could. Jack, have you been hit? You look sort'a pale, sickly like. Do you need help, boy?"

Don cracked a smile. "Wadn't us what done it. It was Jack, here, and he was the only one what got off a shot. Draw'd on one that already had his gun out, and beat the other'n 'fore he knowed it was coming. Faster'n all get out, is what he is." Don's large front teeth made him look a lot like a over grown Jackrabbit, or as Janice thought, a jackass.

"Well, Jack, that was fine shooting. These two fellers and four more robbed the bank over at White Oaks this morning. When they split up, we followed these two. We'll slap them belly down on their horses and take 'em to Lincoln with us. They're part of the Bristol gang, and they've all got a thousand-dollar reward on each of their heads. For these two, it's yours Jack. When you get ready, just ride over to Lincoln and I'll be waiting. We'll walk over to the bank together and have the banker fill your hands. How does that sound to you?" Pat had dismounted and was looking down at the dead men.

"Just fine, Sheriff Garrett, but do you think you could just drop it off at Mr. McFarland's bank, the next time you're in Analla? I'd sure be thankful."

"Sure thing, Jack. Well, we'd better get these fellers loaded and hit the trail. We've got a long ride before dark."

By ten o'clock the next morning, when the planting was all done, Don and Eldon saddled up to head for home. Eldon leaned from his horse, and in a timid voice said, "Jack, when Janice gets back, you be sure and tell her I was asking. In a couple more years she'll be ready for marrying up with."

Janice turned as red as a beet, but held her tongue. "I'll be sure and tell her, Eldon. But I think she's got her heart set on something else."

"Well, you tell her anyway. She sure gave me the eye pretty good the last time I saw her in church." Eldon's smile reached from ear to ear.

"Most certainly did not!" Janice blurted out.

"Huh, what did you say?" Eldon looked stunned.

"Oh, I meant I certainly didn't know she did that sort of thing yet. You know, as young as she is, and all." Janice was openly embarrassed.

Eldon and Don rode off in a slow lope. Janice looked after them until they rode from sight. "Me marry! My foot, I won't be fifteen for another month! Boy, I almost goofed that time. Him sweet on me! I've never heard of anything so ridiculous, and dumb, plumb stupid! He wouldn't know anything about someone giving him the eye, and I certainly wouldn't do it!"

Another two weeks passed before Janice had to make another trip to town for supplies. Her first stop was the bank. As she walked through the door, Mr. McFarland got up from his desk and met her half way, with his hand out, saying, "Jack, my boy! Good to see you. Sheriff Garrett was in and told me about you getting those two men from the Bristol gang. I guess any bank robber will think twice before coming around here looking to rob a bank. At least when the word gets about. Oh, Sheriff Garrett deposited two thousand dollars into the McCord account. Your father's account was all right, wasn't it? I mean, being it's the same family and all." He was all smiles.

Before saying a word, Janice walked over and spit in one of the large brass spittoons. With her thumbs stuck in her back pockets, she said, "Yes, Sir, that was fine. That's the first reward money I ever got, and just wanted to make sure it got to a safe place, and in the McCord account."

"It sure did, and I'll bet your father is going to be mighty proud of you, and of course your mom and Janice too. We should be looking for them back about anytime now, shouldn't we?" His whole face was a question. "They've been gone a good spell."

"As far as I know. But I haven't heard nary a word from them. Well, I'd best be getting my supplies and get on back home. I can't be away from the ranch too awful long, with Dad gone. Work sure does seem to pile up fast when you're by yourself. Seems as if I'm always behind and I'll never catch up. It seems like work is all I do."

"I'll bet it does, my boy. But the Rogers boys were in town Saturday and said you were doing a mighty fine job at keeping all your chores done. Also said you were fast as greased lightning with that .45. Said you took both those men in less than a heart beat and a half." McFarland was proud of Jack.

"Yes, Sir, but most of that was probably luck. They wasn't expecting a kid to draw his gun against one already drawn." Touching the brim of her hat, she said, "Have a nice day, Sir. I'd best be off."

Getting the buckboard, Janice drove up in front of the mercantile. Talking to herself half out loud, she sat a moment, mumbling. Mr. McFarland had stepped out on the walkway, watching her. "If that boy's blond hair was long, you wouldn't know him from his twin sister. Pretty kids, uh huh, sweet."

He hollered down the street. "Jack, is anything wrong? You look kind of pale. Maybe even nervous."

"Oh, no, Sir. I was just trying to remember what supplies I was supposed to get." Janice got five hundred rounds of .45 shells and three hundred rounds of .44s. That should be plenty. She got more groceries thanever before. She wasn't coming back to town for anything at all. If she did have to have something, she would ride horseback over to Lincoln. It was getting hard to find answers when people started asking about her folks.

It had been a little over two months since her family was killed. Today, July the twenty first, was Janice's fifteenth birthday. She woke up crying. "Mama, I need you so bad! What am I going to do? I have no one. Jack, and Daddy, I sure do miss y'all. I'm lonesome most of the time, and do most of my talking to the horses. Maybe I should think about getting a couple more dogs. No, I can't do that, because today, my fifteenth birthday, I start looking for the Kraymons. So happy birthday, Janice McCord!" She washed her face and looked from the kitchen window into the pre-dawn light.

"What am I going to do with the animals? They will have to be taken care of! What am I going to do about the ranch and house? Oh God, I must be crazy, out of my mind, thinking I can just up and leave everything! Please..., please, God, help me!"

Janice cried all the way through breakfast. This wasn't the way birthdays were supposed to be, not alone at fifteen. She went to the barn and the pungent smell of hay and horses calmed her thoughts. She had just started taking care of the animals, when she heard a horse blow through its nose. She froze for just a moment, then drew her .45, and looked from the barn door.

There on one of the prettiest horses she had ever seen, sat the prettiest boy she had ever seen. He looked to be about nineteen or twenty and had dark wavy hair. His well-worn hat was hanging on his back, by a string around his neck. God, but he was pretty. Janice walked out and asked, "Looking for something, Mister?" She tried her best not to sound like a girl.

"Oh, yes, Sir. Is your father around?"

"No, and don't call me, sir. I'm not as old as you are. He and Mom have gone on a trip, and won't be back for awhile. Can I do anything? I mean help in anyway." She wanted to ask him to get down. Her heart thumping, and she wondered if he could see it through her shirt. Also, she noticed her knees getting weak and her palms started to sweat.

"Naw, I guess not. I'm just passing through, and looking for a job. I'm right good at farming and ranching, both." Disappointment covered his face.

Janice smiled, "God did hear me after all. Are you hungry?"

"Yeah, I haven't eaten a bite since early yesterday morning. God did what? Did you say something about God?"

"You wouldn't understand, but get down and come on in. I can fix you something to eat while we talk. I do need help around here for a while."

"Think we could feed my horse first? He ain't eat since I have."

"Go ahead and stall him. You can see the hay and grain. I'll go on in and start your breakfast. When you're done, come on in." Sticking out her hand, Janice said, "By the way, I'm Jack McCord."

"Howdy, Jack. I'm Jim Woodard." He smiled, showing perfect white teeth. Janice got weak in the knees, Eldon could never do this to her.

While Janice was fixing his food, Jim came in and sat at the table. She handed him coffee, saying, "Why don't you tell me something about yourself, Jim? I need help around here until my folks get back. I've got to be gone for about a week or ten days, and need someone to take care of the chores."

"It don't sound like much of a job, but right now anything will help."

"I can pay forty a month, and keep, for you and your horse. This could work out to be permanent. That depends on how you hold up to your work."

"Forty a month! Gosh dang, I didn't know they paid that much out this way, or I'd been here quicker. Are you sure you can hire, and pay me that? I mean, you're pretty young to be doing the hiring." He looked up from his plate of ham and eggs.

Janice's cute little jaws torqued tight. "My folks have been gone for better than two months, and God only knows how much longer! There's a lot of work to be done around here! Do you want the job or not?" She poured more coffee, glaring. She wanted to scream and cry, but didn't. "I do need help. It'll be you or somebody else!"

"Heck, yeah, I'll take it. But when do you have to leave?"

"Today. I'll show you the day to day chores, the rest you can figure out. If you've been around farms and ranches, you shouldn't have any trouble.

There's plenty of food for you, and feed for the animals. I shouldn't be gone much more than a week, or ten days at the most."

After breakfast Janice showed Jim all he was to do while she was gone.

"Now, Jim, you have to watch that little black heifer over there. She's had the scours on and off for a month. I think her mother's milk is too rich. If you have to, take her off milk completely. One other thing, no matter what else you do, don't feed hay from that pile down in the orchard. There's plenty up here in both the barns."

Janice saddled Jack's blazed face, sorrel mare, then went to her bedroom and got a hundred and fifty dollars. She took ten of that and showed Jim where she was putting it, just in case he needed money for something.

Janice put her bedroll and rain slicker behind her saddle, then turned to Jim. "Jim, please don't let me down. I'm depending on you more than you will ever know. If anyone comes around asking questions, tell them you don't know nothing. I should be back no later than ten days from today."

Jim reached up and shook her hand. "Jack, don't you worry about a thing. You'll think you were here along. You won't be missed." He grinned.

"I'd better be missed, I run this place!" Janice by-passed Analla and took the Rio Bonito fork out of the Rio Hondo Valley. The mountains were beautiful this time of year. The small amount of rain they had gotten, sure helped. Winters' snows were long gone, and everything was pretty and green. She felt behind the saddle and was glad she had her rain slicker. Heavy clouds were building over the higher peaks to the south and west. It could rain. It would do the country a world of good if it did.

Over the past couple of months she had ridden Jack's horse almost every day, but her bottom was so tired she didn't know how much longer she could sit in the saddle. She would top a rise, and look around, trying to get her bearings. She was sure this was the trail to Lincoln, Pat Garrett's town.

Looking Lincoln's main street over, Janice saw, and went into McSweeny's Mercantile. A very nice lady eyed her and asked, "May I help you with something, young man? You look kind'a lost."

"No Ma'am, I'm not lost, and yes, Ma'am, I need your help. I need five pounds of beef jerky and a sack of those hardtacks. I'll also need two, one quart canteens."

"My, my. You must be traveling a long way. You know, we've still got a good batch of elk jerky, if you'd like it."

"No, Ma'am. The beef is all right."

As Janice paid for her supplies, Sheriff Garrett walked in and asked for a plug of tobacco. "Well, howdy, Jack. What brings you over this'a way?"

"I'm riding over to Socorro to look at a bull for my dad."

"You be sure and keep a watchful eye. I've heard the Kraymons have joined up with the Bristol gang. And may be in this area, or Fort Sumner."

"Really! I thought they were in Silver City!" Janice was worried.

"Yeah, that's where some of them will be found."

"Say, Sheriff Garrett, if I's to want to ride down to Silver City one of these days, which would be my best route? From here, that is."

"Well, if it was me going, I'd cut due west and a little north of here, right through the edge of the mountains. Its pretty rough, but it'll take you through Three Rivers where you can water your horse, and refill your canteen. After you leave Three Rivers, there ain't much water. Of course this time of year, the rains have filled a few holes. From there you head between Salinas and Skillet Peaks, there's a pass that ain't too bad to cross. Then you cut northwest until you hit the Rio Grande. After you get to Hillsboro, the road's pretty good. But even I'd be careful of road agents going that way."

"Thank you, Sheriff. I'll remember that." She smiled to herself.

Chaptet Four

Sheriff Garrett bought Janice's breakfast and walked with her to the livery for her horse. She paid the hostler four bits and thanked him for the good care of her horse. The hostler was a burly man with snow-white hair. "Nice looking sorrel you have here, boy. Looks like you take right good care of her. Wouldn't be for sale, would she?"

"No, Sir! But thanks for everything. I'll see you again."

Pat Garrett reached out and shook Janice's hand. "Now Jack, you ride easy in the saddle. It's a long way to Socorro, and don't trust nobody!"

"Thank you, Sir. I might see you again on my way back through here."

Janice kicked her horse into an easy lope, and headed west. Pat turned to the hostler and said, "You know, Martin, that boy has been brung up right. Sure is polite, and will make a good man one of these days."

"Yep, noticed that right away. He takes mighty good care of that horse. You can always tell by that." The hostler watched, after Janice until she rode from sight.

Riding north of Sierra Blanca Peak, Janice could see where the tree line stopped, and green scrubs and tall grass took their place. Four hours later she topped a mountain and could see at least fifty miles across and maybe seventy up and down a valley. "Wow! Look at all that snow over there at the foot of the next mountain range! I sure thought it would all be gone by this time of year." Shivering at the thought of no heavy coat, she believed it to be the most beautiful sight she had ever seen.

"There looks to be a lot of desert between here and there, though."

Going down the west side of the mountain was dangerous. It was so steep in places she had to hold on to the back of her saddle with her right hand, just to keep from sliding over the horse's head. The horse was on her back legs, and rump more than once, sliding. Janice held her breath forever.

By the middle of the afternoon, the green of the mountains had turned to desert brown. All she saw was tall mesquite trees, short green bushes, shorter brown grass, and plenty of cactus. Riding into the Three Rivers Ranch headquarters, she saw several cowboys standing with one foot upon the bottom fence rail of the corral, watching another cowboy ride a bucking horse.

A fellow who looked to be in his sixties hollered out, "Step down, Son. Water that horse and rest a might! You wouldn't want the next try at that bronc in the corral, would you?" He gave a broad, ear to ear grin.

"No, thank you, Sir. I just need to water my horse and fill my canteens, if that will be okay. Then I'll be on my way." The words were no more than out of her mouth, when the fellow riding the bronc was thrown over the fence, in a fog of flying dust.

Dust was so thick, Janice could hardly see him, but he was on hands and knees, trying to get up. The man who had been talking to her, walked over and kicked him right in the rear end. "Get your butt back up there and ride that hoss, 'fore he thinks he can't be rode!" The man and other cowboys whooped and hollered, as the fellow started over.

With eyes as big as a dollar, Janice dismounted, and the man walked over and patted her sorrel on the shoulder. "Where might you be headed, son? I see you scrapped the hide off that horse's hocks, sliding down the mountain. I've seen that a time or two before."

"I'm headed over to Silver City." Janice eyed him from the corner of her eye. Why was he so interested in where she was going?

"Fair piece for a youngster to be traveling alone, ain't it?" The man waited for Janice to answer, and when none came, he stuck out his hand. "Lester French. This is my outfit. That was my son I kicked in the rear end."

Janice reached for his hand. "Howdy, Mr. French. I'm Jack McCord."

"Wouldn't happen to be the son of Henry McCord, would you?"

"Yes, Sir, I am." Janice tried recalling if she had ever seen him before.

"Running away from home, are you?" There was that big grin again.

"No, Sir! I'd never do that! I'm just going over to Silver City, business. Should be back through here in about a week. If everything goes right."

"Ever been this way before?" He watched as she filled both canteens.

Pointing to the west, Mr. French said, "You see them peaks over there thirty or so miles? You head a little north of due west and you'll hit a good sized water hole." Looking at the gun on Janice's hip, he added, "mighty young to be toting iron, ain't you, son?" He arched one eyebrow.

"Yes, Sir. But Pa thought it best for this trip. Thanks for the water, I'd best ride." Janice rode out in a long lope, talking to herself. "Why do men think everything is their business, and ask so many stupid questions? 'Where are you going? Why are you going? Why are you riding alone? Kind'a young, ain't you? Mighty big gun for such a little kid, ain't it?' My God, don't they realize they're being nosy? I was just about to run out of answers. I'd hated to have had to gut shoot him so I could leave." She laughed out loud, then giggled. "I wouldn't have done that!"

After a couple of miles she slowed the horse to a walk, and looked at her back trail. Nothing was moving, but she could still see the tall green trees back at the ranch. "I guess I shouldn't feel this way. He really was a nice man, just nosy as all get out." She laughed out loud again and scared her horse.

This was the first time Janice had ever been out in the real desert. Her father had told her some about it, but she never realized how it would look. Mesquite, cactus, and bear grass (yucca) was all she could see. A few tuffs of grass tried to grow here and there among marble sized gravel and sand so hot you couldn't walk on it very far.

She was probably five miles from the pass when she rode upon the water hole, Mr. French had told her about. She watered the horse and made camp for the night.

She laughed at herself, upon finding that the white stuff she had seen from the mountain top wasn't snow, but white sand dunes over sixty feet high. She was very disappointed, but glad she hadn't asked Mr. French, "how far is it to all that snow?" Boy, would that have ever showed her up as dumb. "Wonder how this sand got so white?"

Evidently this water hole was used regularly by travelers. Rocks were piled for a campfire, and the sight looked well used. Where horses had been tied, everything was trampled down to white sand. Janice looked close at the water, it looked fresh and drinkable, and most of all it didn't stink. If little green moss and other larger things were growing in it, Janice wouldn't have even let the horse drink. But where did it come from? There were no rivers or creeks around. To herself, she mumbled, "It can't be rain water, there are no washes coming off the mountains, and it's not muddy. Maybe it's a fresh water spring bubbling up right in the middle, and I can't see it."

She dipped her hand and brought it to her mouth. It was tepid, but good and sweet. Removing the saddle she gave her horse a rub down and fed him, before looking for firewood. She had to walk pretty far for scantily, scattered dead scrub bushes of sage and mesquite. It took well over an hour to get four armloads. She had a fire going just before dark, and lay out her bedroll. She was drinking water and eating jerky when she heard horses blowing through their noses and coming her way. Standing, she touched the butt of her .45, and lifted it a bit in the holster. "This is all I need, company!"

Two horsemen pulled up about a hundred feet away. One of the men stood in his stirrups and spoke loudly. "Howdy, the fire! Can we ride in?"

"Sure thing, ride on in, there's plenty of room." Janice stepped over her bedroll, walking a few steps forward.

The men dismounted and extended their hands for a shake. The largest and older of the two said, "Weldon Rose. This here's Pete Bristol. We've been riding a far piece since sunup. Glad to see your fire."

Janice stuck out her hand. "Jack McCord." Her mind registered, 'Bristol gang'. She'd have to keep an eye on Pete. Maybe he knew she killed those men back at the ranch. Someone could have told them.

The men removed their saddles and flopped them down across the fire from Janice's bedroll. Pete Bristol had been eyeing the sorrel, and Janice's low slung .45. Janice was scared, but felt a little cocky. She remembered what Sheriff Garrett had said. 'Don't trust anyone!' Weldon looked all right to her. He looked clean and well kept, with neatly trimmed beard that was mostly white. To Janice, he just seemed easy going. But... she was about half-afraid of Pete. He was dirty and had little snake eyes that were pinched together over a broken nose. He smelled as bad as the two Bristol men she had killed.

Janice lay awake with her eyes open as long as she could. It was close to midnight when sleep finally overtook her. The smell of wood smoke, and a stronger smell of coffee brewing awakened her. She jumped and grabbed for her .45. Both men were up and had a morning fire going, with coffee on.

"Jack, do you drink coffee?" Weldon had a cup in his hand, and was offering it to Janice. He had a smile on his face.

"Thank you, Sir. I'm just now getting in the habit of drinking coffee."

Pete mouthed off. "Yer too young to have any habits. Where are your folks? What are you doing out here on the trail by yerself, nohow, boy?"

"I'm minding my own business, Sir!" Janice was tired of men being so gosh darned nosy, and was very short with her answer.

Pete's face turned hard, and his eyes narrowed even more than they already were. "You saying I'm nosy, kid?" His voice was as hard as his face.

"Yes, Sir, I'm saying just that." She had a little smirk on her face.

"Well, if you ain't a polite little devil. We'll just see how polite you are when I ride off on that sorrel mare." Pete laughed a long, hard laugh.

Weldon hadn't said a word. He just looked from Pete to Janice, and back again. With coffee in his left hand, he took a long sip, and touched the butt of his gun with his right fingers.

Janice stood with her little feet spread a few inches. "Mister, what would a dead man want with such a good horse?" There wasn't a quiver in her voice, it sounded more like a low growl. Her eyes were as cold as death itself.

Pete turned to face her. "What are you talk'n about kid? What dead man?" He had a dumb, puzzled look on his face.

Weldon quickly poured the rest of his coffee on the fire and stood up, knowing what was about to happen. Janice hadn't moved, but shot right back. "You'll be the dead man, if you even think of touching my horse. I'll kill you where you stand!" The calmness of her voice made Pete look into her eyes. They were cold as blue steel. Not one muscle had twitched on that baby face.

Pete roared out with a dirty, hard, laugh. "Now if that don't sound like gun-slinger talk to me, I don't know what is! Weldon, to make this fair, I'm going to let this gun-slinging kid go first. What do you think? Think I can beat this bad man? Haw, haw. Looks plumb nasty to me. I mean, I do want to make it fair." But still..., his loud talk hadn't washed away that small cloud of doubt.

Weldon stepped away from the fire. "Pete, you try to take the kid, and you've got me first. You don't gun down the man that let you share his fire, and then go and steal his horse. It just ain't done." Weldon touched his beard with his left hand, but his right was dangling just below his gun butt.

Janice had a good idea what was about to happen, as she listened to Pete brag on. "Weldon, old boy, I never liked you nohow, always thinking you was better'n me. You know damned well I do what I want to."

Pete grabbed for his gun, but was a might slow. Weldon's bullet took him straight in the chest. Kicking out the hull, and inserting a fresh cartridge, Weldon said, "That man's needed killing for a mighty long time. Don't you worry none, Jack. Long's I'm around, nobody'll do you no harm."

"Thanks for your help, Weldon. I just knew he wasn't taking my horse. Look at the crow-bait he rode in on. He sure didn't take care of that one."

"Jack, I'm not being nosy, or nothing like that, but are you in some kind of trouble? Like running from home?" By the sound of his voice, Janice thought he was concerned, and probably worried about her, thinking her a him.

She looked at him for a moment, then turned and picked up her saddle. Was he being nosy, or was he really concerned? As she walked to her horse, she asked over her shoulder, "why would you ask a thing like that? Do I look as if I'm running from the law?" She snickered out loud.

Weldon gave out a gentle laugh, and walked away from camp about twenty feet. With his back to Janice, he proceeded to take a leak. Janice blushed and turned to her horse. Weldon started talking over his shoulder.

"Jack, again, I don't mean to embarrass you, but I heard you crying in your sleep last night."

Janice turned red, but was on the other side of her horse, away from Weldon. "Yeah, well sometimes I just do that! While you're finishing with y'all's camp, I'd better go out behind them bushes. You know, so the next traveler won't come along and step in something and get mad."

"Yeah, go ahead. I'll get Pete loaded belly down on his horse. May as well take him into Hillsboro. What do you think?" It's still a two day ride."

"I think he would be stinking even worse than he does now. I think we should take him over beside one of them big old mesquite trees and cover him with sand. I'd hate to take him with us, and then the word get around we killed him. I don't think I can kill very many more of the Bristol gang, and get away with it, As nasty as Pete was, I figgered y'all already knew."

Weldon turned around with his eyes narrowed. "What do you mean, 'kill any more of the Bristol gang'? I killed Pete, you didn't."

"Yeah, but I killed two of them a few weeks ago. After that bank job over at White Oaks, they came by our place and tried taking two of our horses. I didn't let them do it. Sheriff Garrett buried them in Lincoln."

"That was you! Remind me never to try and take one of your horses. So you'll know, Jack. I've never rode with them boys. Know 'em, that's all."

"Thanks for telling me that, Weldon. Well, I'd best take care of business so we can get Pete buried. I'll be back in a bit." Janice had never come so close to wetting her pants as now. She wondered if walking cross-legged would help until she was out of sight of Weldon. But what would she do on the trail with Weldon along? She'd think of something, even if she had to ride off the trail to look at a odd rock outcropping, or something else strange.

"You go ahead, Jack. I'll take care of Pete. After all, he was with me."

It was late in the afternoon when they reached the Rio Grande. And it was a very hot and dry July day. Riding under tall cottonwood trees to the river's edge, Weldon got off his horse and sat on a log. Removing his boots, he looked over at Janice. "Come on, Jack. Take them clothes off and let's hit that water. Boy, it sure looks cool." Weldon was already unbuttoning his shirt. He had the right idea about cooling down.

"Uh, naw, you go ahead. I think I'll go back among the trees and find me a nice spot to take me a nap." Janice was already blushing.

Weldon laughed, "Not afraid of the water, are you?"

"Naw, I just never learned to swim." She lied again, and hated it.

Weldon laughed again. "That's wise, Jack. Stay out of the water until you learn how to swim. You go on and nap, I'm gonna soak for an hour."

Janice ground tied her horse, and walked back in the woods a little way. There she did her business, then moved closer to the river and lay in the shade. Weldon walked up with his boots and pants on, but no shirt. "Hey, Jack, what do you say to making camp here for the night? Only a couple more hours until sundown, and this is a lot better spot than somewhere out on the trail, and having a dry camp." He was strapping on his gun, as he spoke. Then pulled his gun from the holster and checked it's load.

"Sounds good to me. I'm bone tired and my rump feels like it's asleep. I think I'll catch a little more shut-eye, then get up and think about fixing something to eat." Janice lay back and wanted to rub her bottom, but didn't.

Weldon chuckled out loud. "You go ahead and rest. I'll walk out here a ways and get us a rabbit for supper. When you hear my gunfire, don't panic."

Late the next afternoon they rode into Hillsboro on tired horses. After putting the horses in the livery, Weldon said he was hitting the saloon for a stiff drink and a few hands of poker. Janice laughed, "Yeah, I would too, but I'm just a little young for that. I'm headed for a bath and bed. I stink so bad it's spooking my horse."

Janice went to the hotel and got herself a room. "I'll need hot water for my bath. As soon as possible, if you don't mind."

"It'll be right up, young man."

Janice waited until the water boy left, then locked the door. She walked over and got a chair and put it under the doorknob. After taking off her clothes she stepped into the hot water. "God, I've needed this!" She soaked until the water got cold before getting out and drying off. She lay naked on the bed for a couple of minutes before remembering she was naked. Jumping up she put her clothes on. "Lord, what would I have done if someone had knocked on the door? Died, that's what I'd done! I would have just dropped dead and they'd found me laying here on the floor naked!"

Janice was down for breakfast by five o'clock. She sat alone eating, but just as she was about to leave, Weldon walked in.

"Good morning, Jack. Sleep good in that soft bed?"

"Yeah, I sure did. But, I guess I'm about ready to hit the trail."

"Well, myself, I just got out of a poker game. I think I'll get me a room and sleep all day. Say, do you need a little money? I sure made me a gob in that game, and can spare a little if you need it." He saw her eyes narrow, and quickly added, "I mean just until we meet up again on some trail. Then you could pay me back. You know, Jack, sort'a a loan. I sure got more than I'll need for awhile."

"Thanks, Weldon, but I've got all I'll need. Before I go, why did you befriend me against Pete? Then ride along with me to make sure I'd get safely this far? Then offer to loan me money? Care to tell me why you'd do that?" She stood by the table, waiting.

Weldon's face got long. "Yeah, I reckon I can tell you the reason why. I got a son about your age. Hope he's looked after. He's back east. Ain't seen him since he was ten," Janice stood and looked down into Weldon's face. Sticking out her hand, she said, "Weldon, you're a good man to ride the trail with. I sure hope to meet up with you again sometime. You are all right in my book. Few men would have done what you did."

Weldon stood, "You too, boy, and we will meet up again. Now you ride easy like in the saddle. Very few fellers out there like you and me. Don't let none of 'em hurt you. And remember, Jack, don't trust nobody!" He smiled.

Janice went to the livery for her horse. When she started to pay for its keep, the hostler said, "Mr. Rose was by a little bit ago and has already taken care of your feed bill. Said for me not to charge you nary a dime. He sure is a nice feller, huh, young man?" He handed Janice the reins to her horse.

"Yes, Sir, he sure is." Janice mounted and headed toward Silver City. Thinking of Weldon, she wondered what he did for a living. "Maybe he's a big time gambler. Or maybe he's a gunfighter, killer. He sure was fast with his gun when he killed Pete. I wonder if I'll ever be that fast? I probably gotta be, to get them Kraymons."

Two days later she rode past the Gila Copper Mines and was told it was nine miles to Silver City. Pulling up in front of the livery, she handed the hostler the reins, and asked, "Mister, can you tell me the closest hotel and the worst saloon? " Janice stood with a funny little look on her face, and started to lower her eyes away from his, but didn't. She had her hands on her hips.

"I can tell you, Sonny, but you be careful. Them old boys are meaner'n a sick dog. Go south a block and a half. It's next door to the whorehouse."

Janice blushed at the word 'whorehouse,' but said, "Thanks, Mister."

"You take your time, Son. It's four bits a day, with grain for the horse."

Janice got herself a room and cleaned up before walking down to the saloon. Never had she been in such a place. Everyone was talking at once, and the music was so loud, she wondered why anyone would even try to talk. The stink made her want to gag. Never had she smelled a cow lot that was worse than this. The smell of tobacco, whiskey, beer, and rotten puke, along with stinking bodies was enough to turn her stomach. Ten feet inside the door, she stopped to look around. The bartender hollered at her. "What do you want in here, kid? Come 'ere!" He had a gruff voice, but a friendly smile. "Son, this ain't a good place for a kid like you to be. Want a beer?" He grinned. "Er maybe a shot of whiskey?"

Janice tried not to giggle, but did. "Naw, I'll have a sarsaparilla, Sir."

"One sarsaparilla coming up!" He smiled and said, "that'll be a nickel, if you got one. If you don't, it's still a nickel, but I'll pay for you."

"Thank you, Sir, but here's my money."

"Kind'a polite little feller for being in a place like this, ain't you?"

"Yes, Sir." Janice took a sip of her drink, and found it a bit bitter.

"I'm Bob Hamblin." The bartender was overly inquisitive. "You do got a name, don't you?" Two men down the bar started hollering for service.

Sticking her hand across the bar, Janice said, "Howdy, Bob Hamblin. I'm Jack McCord." She relaxed a bit, and smiled.

"All right, now that I know you, what are you doing here?"

The smile left her face. "Looking for the Kraymons."

"That's one of them, standing ten feet down the bar from you."

There were two men standing together, and had been eyeing Janice. As soon as Bob went over to wait on someone else, they started in on her. One was an ugly, pimpled face, buck-toothed kid who looked about nineteen. The other man was older, and really had a loud mouth. Janice thought she recognized him as a Kraymon.

Moving down the bar a little closer to Janice, he bellowed out, "Kind'a young being in here, ain't ya kid? You look pretty enough to have to squat to pee. Boy, if you had long hair to go along with them full lips, I'd bed you down anyway." Both men roared in laughter, waiting and watching for Janice's reaction. But neither was expecting what they got. Which was a lot more than they bargained for.

As Janice stepped away from the bar, then slowly moved to her left, while wishing the light was better in here. "You wouldn't happen to be a Kraymon, would you?" Janice was ready to draw. She had centered her weight over both legs. Kraymon knew a drawing stance, and stepped back.

"Whoa, there! Yeah, I'm Ed Kraymon! Do I know you, kid?" He looked surprised, but didn't step closer in the dim light for a better look at Janice.

Janice wanted to scream her words, but calmly answered, with much emphasis. "Yeah, you know me! You also knew my mother and father. Henry and Alice

McCord. Don't stand there looking plumb stupid! You know, the McCord ranch, a little east of Analla! You raping, murdering polecat!"

"Jack McCord! But, but, Sam killed you! I saw you fall face down!"

"Wrong!" Through clinched teeth, she hissed, "I'm Janice McCord, and have come to kill you!" Janice watched as Ed moved away from the bar.

It never crossed either one of their minds, that they would be the one to lose this deadly duel. Ed half snickered with a frightful look of contempt, not fear. "Dumb assed kid!" Ed went for his gun, but before he cleared leather, he knew he was dead. Janice shot him in the face, and as he fell back, she shot him three times in the groin as fast as she could pull the trigger. "That's for Jack, and my mom and dad, you no good yeller bellied, women murdering polecat!" She stood above him with her gun still smoking in her right hand.

The younger fellow hadn't moved from the bar, as he knew Ed would take this kid out in a blink of an eye. When he saw Ed go down, he started for his gun, but Janice still had hers in her hand. "Mister, I didn't come here to kill you, but if you make a move for that gun, you're as stupid and as dead as he is!" Unblinking, she held his stare, eye for eye, as though daring him to go for his gun. She would kill him too.

The sheriff came slamming through the bat-wing doors of the saloon. His gun was in his right hand, and cocked. "All right, Billy! What are you...?"

He looked at the body lying on the floor. "My God, you've gone and killed Ed! You're rotten to the core, Billy Bonny! Your friend, and you went and killed him!" Sheriff Boggs was mad as hell.

"Look at that! Why in the hell did you shoot him in crotch? You know undertaker George don't like that shit. Damn, it's just too stinkin', messy!"

"Hold your damn horses, just a minute, Boggs! I didn't do nothing! Ed was talking with this kid. The next thing I knowed he was going for his gun. He didn't make it, the kid out draw'd him." The whole room was quiet.

The sheriff turned to Janice. "You out draw'd Ed! What the hell kind of a joke is this? Son, if you're siding with this lying little bastard, because you're afraid of him... Janice cut him off in mid-sentence.

"Sheriff, I ain't afraid of any man alive! And I killed Ed Kraymon, because I'm faster than he was. Him and his four brothers gunned down my family. That was over at Analla about two and a half months ago. They raped my mother before putting a gun to her heart and pulling the trigger. Ed was only the first, I've got four more Kraymons to go, and kill them all, I will!" "Son, Son, young gunslingers don't last. And that might be again the law. It could be, you know." He turned to Billy Bonny.

"What about it Billy? What did you see? Ed was fast with a gun, better'n any kid! If you've gone and pulled a fast one…!"

Billy threw the rest of a hot beer down his throat, and swaggered over to the Sheriff. "The kid's telling it straight, Boggs. Ed went first. I saw it all."

Boggs looked Janice straight in the eyes. "All right, kid, but it'd be best if you hit the trail. Ed has a lot of friends around Silver City. They'll be wanting to make it right. Billy here is one of them. They'll pick a fight, then call it self-defense. This is William Bonny, he calls hisself, Billy the Kid. Watch your back around him, ain't that right, Billy? Murdering little shit!"

"You know better'n that Sheriff, or you'd already hung me. Right?"

"Yeah, you're right, but one of these days you'll step over that thin line. And when you do, some lawman will hang you high, or shoot you down."

The Sheriff turned to Janice. "Young man, you'd better go. I can't be around to protect you all night. I got other saloons to look after."

"Thanks Sheriff, you're right. But can you tell me if any more of the Kraymons are in town? I'd sure like to have me a talk, or at least say hello to a couple more of them, before I head back home."

"I can tell you, and they're not. They've gone to Fort Sumner, I think."

"Thanks, Sheriff, I'll just finish my sarsaparilla and go on to the hotel. I'll be leaving at sunup. I've got a long ride."

The undertaker walked in the door and started cussing the instant he saw Ed's crotch. "Why in the hell does anybody shoot anybody between the legs? It just don't make any sense! Shit, blood and guts all over the damn floor! Bob, you'll have to get somebody to clean up after this. Damn flies will be after that blood and shit any minute now."

The bartender told him what had happened, then turned to Janice. "Son, that wasn't a wise thing to do, going and killing Ed. I can't watch your back, so you walk with eyes in the back of your head all the way to the hotel. Somebody's bound to try and back shoot you, ain't that right, Billy? You'll answer to me if you do! Get that stupid look off your face! Little asshole!" It was easy to tell that Bob Hamblin didn't like Billy the Kid.

"I won't do it, Bob. Naw, not me. I just want to talk with the kid for a minute. That's all right, ain't it?" His smile made him even uglier.

"As long as talk is all you do. Listen good, Billy! No trouble!"

Billy stuck out his hand to Janice. "Billy the Kid's what ever'body calls me. Bet they call you pretty boy, or something sissified like that, huh.?"

"Jack McCord is what everyone calls me, and you're as ugly as where my dog last took a dump! Anybody ever tell you that? If Ed Kraymon was your friend, and evidently he was, you can tell his brothers that one of the McCords lived. I'll come looking for them in my own sweet time. They will die, by my gun." Janice spoke with conviction in her voice, but low and even, unwavering. "And anybody else that tries to stop me from doing it, will die."

"Tell you what, kid. I'll just take you out tonight, then they won't have to worry about it. What do you say to that?" A sneer flickered across his face.

Janice stepped away from the bar again. "I think you'd be dead before you cleared leather, and the sawdust on this floor would be soaking up your blood. What do you think of that?" Her eyes were as cold as steel, and not a quiver vibrated her voice. Her hand was even with the gun butt on her hip.

Death was quickly tapping Billy on the shoulder, and got his attention. "Aah, naw, naw thanks. It can wait." The chill that drifted through his body, went all the way from his head to his toes. He needed a drink, bad.

Janice awoke from a deep sleep and looked around the dark room. Something had awakened her, a noise. Seeing a shadow at the window, she rolled from her bed with her .45 in her hand. Moving quietly, she stood beside the window. Moments later it opened without a sound. A man's head stuck through and looked at the bed. Janice brought the barrel of her gun down hard. She looked over the body into the street below. There stood another man holding two horses. Pulling and jerking, Janice got the unconscious man inside her room. Taking his gun, she looked at it, a .44, she couldn't use it, so she stuffed it under the mattress, then got dressed in a minute flat. Glancing back out the window, she saw the other man was still below, and looking nervous. "Stupid goat, they ain't getting me this way! And if they do, it'll take a lot more than two of them!"

Grabbing her things, she bolded out the back door, and down the stairs. Running as fast as she could, she went to the livery. Saddling her horse, she looked around and saw the hostler's coffee cup setting on a post beside the door. Dropping in a dollar before swinging into the saddle, she rode fast out the back door of the livery. She had to head for home.

The creek was only a hundred feet away, so she rode down it headed south. It was still too dark to let the horse run, but she kicked him into a slow lope as soon as they left the water. Getting to the south edge of town, she turned east and headed for home. Pale pink had just brightened the sky.

As pink turned to orange, the sun came over the horizon. She topped a high tree covered hill several miles east of Silver City, then stopped and turned in the saddle.

Looking at her back trail, she saw a dust trail boiling up behind several fast moving horses.

"Boy, there's a bunch of them fellers, and I'll bet they're coming after me. I guess I talked too much in that saloon, they know my trail." Janice left the Hillsboro road and cut southeast toward Fort Bayard. In about three miles she hit the fort road, and kept up a fast gallop until she went through the fort gate. A private stopped her. "What are you doin' here kid?" His manner of talk was snotty, and Janice just wanted to reach out and slap him.

"I wondered if anybody around here could sell me some field glasses?"

The private looked quickly around to see if anyone else might have heard. "I got some. Cost you two dollars, and keep your mouth shut!"

"If you get them in a hurry, like right now, I'll make it three."

The private turned for a building on his left. Janice called to him. "Hey, there'll be an extra four bits if you can bring me a biscuit and a slab of that beef that I smell. I'm starved." Her stomach was growling so loud, she hurt.

Five minutes later the private was back with a small burlap sack. "It's all in here, where's my money?" He held the sack just out of her reach.

Janice held a five-dollar gold piece between her thumb and finger. "You get all of this gold piece if you can tell me what's south of here, and how far. And, can I ride on through the fort and out the back side?"

"Southeast twenty-five miles is the Mimbres River. Another seventy-five miles to the Rio Grande, is Mesilla. Go straight out that back gate." He reached for the gold piece.

Chapter Five

Janice was glad to be riding Jack's horse, which was half quarter horse, and half through-bred from England. It was deep chested and strong, but could hold a hard lope better than any other horse at the McCord ranch. Jack had raced her against several horses around Analla, but none could even come close. It wasn't yet mid-morning when she rode through the water, and up the east bank of the Mimbres River, still heading southeast. The hills she just came through were not nearly as high as the ones she could see a few miles further ahead. She had to make those hills before stopping for a rest, if her bottom would hold out. Her and the horse were sweating profusely.

Staying north of the tallest peak, and riding hard she topped the mountain two hours after crossing the river. Dismounting she let her horse rest awhile, and took a drink from her canteen. Taking her field glasses she eyed her back trail. Seven riders were coming on fast about three quarters of a mile from the base of the mountain. A cold chill ran down Janice's spine.

"Boy, they want me bad! I sure stirred up a stink."

Her hand unconsciously fell to the butt of her .45.

"Let me see now, it should take them at least another hour to make it up this mountain...I hope. My horse needs to rest a little more." Taking the glasses, she looked again, then jumped on her horse and rode for ten minutes before she could see almost forever. Nothing but flat grasslands lay before her as far as the eye could see. "I'm not getting get caught out there!

"I'll just have to make a stand back at that little pass. As narrow as it is, I should be able to at least turn them around. I'll get me the best spot and hold them until nightfall. If there's a full moon tonight, I can be halfway across those flats before they know it." She was suddenly scared, but turned around.

She rode back to the top of the pass, and put her horse completely out of sight. Taking her rifle and fifty shells, she looked around, finding the spot she wanted. She had a clear field of view for over four hundred yards down the pass, and there was no cover for the men. Once they rode into the clearing, they would be wide open to her fire. They would have to ride into her rifle, or turn back. With that many horses, it would be hard to get them turned quickly in that narrow gap. She looked at her hand to see how steady it was. "Not bad for a kid." She tried to laugh, but it didn't come out of her mouth.

Janice watched as the horsemen rode single file up the cut. Walking to her horse she got her canteen and took a big drink of water. She got back to her hiding place just as the men rode onto open ground. Taking a deep breath, she pushed back her hat, and brought the rifle to her shoulder. She could now make out individual faces. Billy the Kid was the third man in line. They were about two hundred yards away when Janice allowed for the drop in altitude and sighted down the barrel before pulling the trigger.

The first man in line was shot in the forehead. His arms and legs went wide as he was knocked backward over his horse's rump. The next horse back stepped right in his face, as the men jerked their reins. Before they could get their thoughts about them, the next man was shot in the left side of his rib cage. He screamed as the shot blew out a rib from each side of his body. By the time he hit the ground, the other men were fighting their horses to get them turned, so they could get back through the narrow gap.

Janice was so scared, she felt her stomach was in her mouth. She hadn't realized how badly she was shaking. How had she held a straight aim? She had jacked another shell into the chamber without knowing it. Opening the breech, she asked herself, "How many shots have I fired? Do I need to reload? Oh, God! Here they come again!" She wiped her palms dry on her pants, and quickly brought her rifle back to her shoulder.

Two men were laying low across their horse's necks, riding as fast as they could up the rocky gap. Janice aimed for the front horse's head and fired. The first horse went head long into the ground. The second horse hit the fallen rider full in the chest with a front hoof, then a hind one. Even with all the noise, the other rider heard the scream of the downed man, as broken ribs punctured both lungs. The fallen rider clutched his chest and died, blood gushing from his lips.

The rider straightened up to turn back, and Janice shot him five inches below the heart. He sagged and grabbed the hole in his chest with one hand, and the saddle horn with the other, then turned his horse back down the gap. Billy had lied to him, he had said a snot nosed kid had killed Ed. He had said nothing about a cold-blooded killer, that didn't miss.

The horse ran from sight with it's rider slumped sideways in the saddle. Janice was oddly calm as she sat reloading her rifle. "That's four of them. That means there are three more to go." She raised her eyes toward heaven. "Thanks for hearing my prayers. Lord, I mean it, thanks."

Janice watched and waited for over half an hour. She started to take a drink from her canteen when she saw three horsemen leading a horse with a man slumped over in his saddle. They were heading back down the mountain. She looked at the sun; it was only noon. "Lord, I'm glad I didn't have to hold that bunch all day." She got a drink, and lay back for just a moment.

Getting her horse, Janice rode down the east side of the pass, and across flat grasslands. She let the horse lope as she glanced over her shoulder at her back trail. If only she had waited a bit longer before riding from the mountain, she would have seen two of the men kick their horses into a run heading south. Billy the Kid took the wounded man back toward Silver City.

Billy kept things going over in his mind. There would be hell to pay for so many dead men. And a snot nosed kid did it.

Janice let the horse lope for over an hour before slowing to a walk. She hoped she would make the next small mountain range before dark. She didn't want to camp out in the open. All afternoon she rode as hard as she thought the horse could take, without wearing her completely out. They were both bone tired, and the sun kept beating down. Stopping, she took a drink from her canteen, then filled her hat and let her horse drink from it. The sun was just a giant red ball, low in the western sky when she rode into a little cove. She had simply lucked out and rode upon a small spring with several trees standing tall. She looked the area over and decided it would be easy to defend, if need be. "Plenty of cover, this will be just fine. I hope."

The horse drank, and she filled her canteens, then moved two hundred feet or so away from the spring area. Janice pushed her horse up a thirty-degree incline to a level spot where there was plenty of grass. Here she lay out her bedroll and would be asleep in nothing flat. She couldn't remember ever being this tired. In fact, if she wasn't this tired, she probably would have just cried herself to sleep. Never had she felt more alone, than now. She figured she might as well get use to it.

The morning light was bright, but the sun wasn't up when her horse blew through it's nostrils and pointed her ears toward the spring. Janice jumped up and pulled her rifle from its boot. Walking easily, she moved to a spot above and north of the spring. There sat two men around a small fire, with coffee on. Janice eased down where she could hear them talking. She thought they might hear her heart beating. She dropped behind a boulder, when a crow cawed above her, as it sailed toward the trees. She sat still for several moments, afraid to breathe out loud. "Stupid crow!"

One of the men was short and kind of pudgy, while the other was tall and had a dark, ugly beard. The short one started talking. "Butch, it don't matter what Billy said about this kid. This little devil can shoot yer eye out at over two hundred yards. And he's got guts, standing against all of us. No running in him. I think we ought'a forget him and get on back to Silver City. We can tell Sam, and let him take care of his own problems." He shook his head up and down, wanting an agreeing answer to all he had said.

"And what do you think Sam Kraymon would do when we told him a snot-nosed kid made us high-tail it for home? I'll tell you, he'd kill us hisself! Naw, this little sucker killed Ed, and I'm going to make it right!"

Janice listened, smelling their breakfast. Boy, was she ever hungry. She jacked a shell into the firing chamber, and left her rifle cocked. Moving ever so slowly, she walked up behind the men.

"Don't move a muscle! The hammer is back and my finger is on the trigger. You on the right, reach over and get his gun with your left hand and pitch it back here." Janice waited until the gun landed in front of her, then she picked it up and stuck it in her belt. Their food sure smelled good.

"All right, face each other. Now you, with your left hand, reach and get his gun and pitch it here. And Mister, when it comes free of that holster, don't try and grab it, or you're dead first! All right, now back up and sit down on that log. And remember, this trigger has a light spring." Janice held her rifle in her right hand with her finger on the trigger. Taking her time, she removed their rifles from their saddle scabbards. Moving twenty feet to her right, she dropped them into the little spring. When her eyes dropped to the splash, the tall man started to lunge forward, toward Janice, so she shot him in the right leg. He dropped to the dirt like a shot buffalo, wallowing around in pain.

"Stupid, is what you are Mister! I didn't want to do that, but you made me! And that shot could have been between your eyes. You! Get over there and tie something around that leg to stop the blood. Believe me, I don't want to kill you, unless I have to. Neither of you a Kraymon, are you?"

"No! Not us, but you killed Ed! That's why we're after you young feller. Before it's over with, one of us will get you." The tall one was down on his left side, while the other man worked on his leg. He was in a lot of pain, but didn't show it in his face. Only his eyes showed hate, but said nothing about it.

"Hey Butch, that slug went plumb through. Looks real clean, didn't bust no bone, or nothing like that." He shook his head up and down.

Butch leaned over and with one eye looked at the wound.

"Did you get the bleeding stopped?" Janice asked as she still held the rifle firm in her hands. "You should clean that wound, after I leave."

"Yeah, looks like it might hold. The bullet just went through flesh."

Janice had the short one pull Butch back against the log they had been sitting on. "I shouldn't take the time, but I'm going to tell you fellers something that might save your lives. The reason I killed Ed Kraymon, is because him and four of his brothers shot down my family. They raped my mother and put a gun to her heart. Kraymons shot my father while he sat tied to a porch rail. My twin was shot in the face while coming to help my mother. Now I am going to kill every one of them Kraymons that was at my house.

"I pray that I won't have to kill many more men like you, but anyone that rides after me, I'll shoot down. I'm sorry about having to kill your friends back there at the pass, but that wasn't the time to talk. I have no idea what Billy the Kid told you men, but now you have the straight story. Please don't follow me anymore. I'll have to kill you if you do. Nothing nor no one will stop me from getting everyone of the Kraymons." She was very matter of fact, and meant it.

Butch, still lying on the ground, looked up and said, "Kid, that ain't the way we heard it. We was told you shot Ed down in cold blood. He didn't even know it was coming. We had no idea about your family, or I'd have shot him myself. I don't know about Roy here, but I won't ride with 'em no more, if you're telling it true. I don't take to killin' women folk er kids, none a'tall. The rest of the Kraymons are in White Oaks, or maybe Fort Sumner. Go get 'em kid! Just wish I could maybe help."

Janice still had her finger on the rifle trigger. "What about you, Roy? Are you coming after me?" Janice watched Roy's plump face, with the beads of sweat trickling down and off his double chin.

"No, Sir, young man. You're letting us ride when you could have let daylight through us. No, of the seven men what took up yore trail, me and Butch have got off easy. Now that little skunk, Billy..., well, me and Butch will have a thing or two to discuss with that young man, next time we see him."

With the rifle still pointed their way, Janice eased back to the spring and got their rifles. Turning them stock up, she drained the water from each one. "I want to believe you, so I'll just put your guns over by that big rock as I ride off. If either of you see the Kraymons, I'd be obliged if you'd tell them I'm coming. They're going to be in a world of hurt, when I find them."

Butch gave a crooked smile and showed his even white teeth. "Well, kid, they'd better hope it's real soon. As good as you are with them guns, God only knows how good you'll be a year from now." Butch leaned back before going on. "You know, Kid, it's strange what a man, or young man, can do when he has to, ain't it?" He leaned on one elbow and looked up at Janice.

"Yes, Sir, it is. And I'm truly sorry about having to shoot you in the leg. I didn't set out to kill nobody but them Kraymons. That is something I have to do. I've waited too long, and still have a long way to go."

"Better being shot in the leg, than between the eyes." Butch chuckled out loud, then grimaced in pain. His ugly beard and hair made him look wild.

"I want to believe you, so good luck to the both of you. I'll be riding, but please don't follow. If you get in range, I'll blow you out of your saddles."

Janice went for her horse, then rode back in view of Roy and Butch. She got off the horse and put their guns in plain sight. Remounting, she touched the brim of her hat, and rode off in a slow lope.

Butch leaned back against the log and said, "Hand me some of that breakfast. You know, Roy, that kid sure cheated the devil today. Kept him from getting either one of us. I've been an outlaw and more than half bad since I was twenty years old. Never looked at the other fellers side of it, 'til now. What that young man did and said today, will change the rest of my life. Way I figger it, we butted into something where we had no business. You know what I mean, we was mad about Ed getting killed, and just went off half cocked. Either one of us would have done what this kid's doing. Our biggest mistake was listening to that lying rat, Billy. That darn near got us killed. We're only twenty miles from Mesilla, and ninety back to Silver City. I'm going to ride into Mesilla and have the doc take care of this leg. Then I'm going to tail after that young feller. Uh huh and the Kraymons. You coming?" He reached for his plate of beans and sourdough bread.

"Yeah, reckon so. Ain't neither of us done no good fer nobody, and we do owe him. 'Sides that, somebody kill my family, I'd try what he's trying."

Two hours after leaving Roy and Butch, Janice rode into Mesilla. The day was only four hours old, but she put her horse in the livery, then went straight to the hotel for breakfast and bed. God but she was hungry and tired.

After sleeping all day, and night, she was ready for breakfast. An hour later she saddled her horse and was on the trail, headed for home. Leaving the Rio Grande Valley behind, she rode east toward the Organ Mountains. As the terrain started a sharp incline up the Saint Augustine Pass, she looked at her back trail. Taking field glasses, she got a better look. Back about three miles, two men seemed to be following her. They looked to be in no hurry as their horses were only in a slow lope. Then still, they were going the same speed as her. Talking to herself, she kicked her horse out a little more.

"Well, this is a stage road, and anybody can come and go as they wish. I'll just keep a better look at my back trail from here on. Its not like they can sneak up on me. Heck fire, I can see for a hundred miles, out here on this desert." Unconsciously she picked up the pace, just a little.

Going down the eastside of the pass, Janice met the westbound stage around mid-morning. It was going slow because of the steep incline. Hollering at the driver, she waved, "How far to the next water hole?"

The shotgun guard shouted back. "Seventeen miles! Bleaker Station!"

Janice loped her horse awhile longer, then slowed as the sun kept beating down, hot. She was riding along the south end of the white sands she came across up north. From this distance, the Sacramento Mountains looked to be dark blue. Haze from the sun beating down on the desert floor, caused heat waves to shimmer and distort everything more than a mile or so away.

Bleaker Station was nothing but a rock building with a horse tank and windmill next to it. Janice ate a good meal, while her horse rested. Twenty minutes later she was in the saddle, and didn't look back for over an hour. Remembering the riders, she looked back to see them loping along behind.

"If that's who I think it is, I should have shot them both! Lying rotten skunks!"

Several miles before Janice got to the Sacramento Mountains, the stage road turned north to the little village of La Luz. She figured she had ridden over seventy miles today. By riding hard tomorrow, she could be home before dark. The livery in La Luz didn't have stalls, and the corral was built from large mesquite limbs that were tied together with yucca spines. She didn't like it, but one night wouldn't hurt. Getting a room at the inn, she found it to have dirt floors, and no lock on the door. The bed was made of the same mesquite limbs as the corral. At least the straw was fresh, and smelled clean.

Janice left the stage road when it turned toward Tularosa. Riding straight north, she would tie back in with it at the base of the mountain. Before riding past Fort Stanton, again she saw the horsemen coming on behind her. "What if it is Butch and Roy? I'll stop off and see Sheriff Norval in Analla. I'll just wait around there until they ride in. I can't let them follow me home."

As she passed Fort Stanton, several soldiers were standing by the road, and spoke. "Howdy." Janice nodded her howdy, then pushed her horse even faster. She had to make it to Analla before dark.

Dismounting in front of Sheriff Norval's small jail, she brushed the trail dust from her pant legs as she walked up the steps. "Howdy, Sheriff."

"Sheriff Norvel looked shocked. "Jack McCord! So, you finally came back to give yourself up! Boy, we had no idea where to start looking for you."

Janice looked at him with a puzzled look. "Give myself up! For what?"

"Why, for murdering your family, and burying them out there in that orchard. You ought'a knowed you couldn't get away with something like that. Shor's hell tried, though, didn't you!"

Janice turned pale, and almost went to her knees. "Me! Murder my family! You're crazy as a mule kicked dog, if you'd think for one minute I'd kill my family!" She was mad that anyone would even think such a thing.

"No sense denying it, Jack. That new hired hand of yours, Jim Woodard found the grave markers. Said they looked about a couple months old. That's when you came to town, and started spending all that money."

"You found the markers, but did you dig up the graves?" Janice asked.

"No, no sense doing that. Your folks have been gone nigh on to three months, and all of y'all's horses are there. No wagon or buggy is missing. You built them markers and put 'em up. No, you done away with them, and will probably hang over at Lincoln when the Circuit Judge gets around again."

Janice backed up and started her hand toward her .45. Jim Woodard had walked up behind her, and before she could draw her gun, he yanked it from her holster. She spun around to face him. Tears welled in her eyes. "Jim! How could you think such a thing, and then help them hang me for something I'd never do?"

"Jack, I'm sorry. But when the cows busted down the fence, I went to rebuild it. That's when I found the covered up markers. I came to the sheriff."

"You're both wrong! Sam Kraymon and his brothers are the ones that killed my family! I just got back from Silver City, where I out gunned Ed."

Sheriff Norval walked back and opened the cell door. "Yeah, in a big fat hogs rump, you out gunned Ed Kraymon. Hand me your gun belt, Jack, and step in here. I'd like to believe you, but all the evidence points right to you. And why would the Kraymons want to kill your family? Maybe you can convince a jury that you're innocent, but not me. You're guilty all right, and tomorrow I'll be taking you to Lincoln." He opened the creaking cell door.

Janice's eyes were red and filled with tears. She wanted to cry and scream, but held her composure and turned to Jim. "Jim, will you at least stay out at the place until they find I'm innocent, or hang me? The animals still need to be taken care of. And all the fields will need watering. You know, all the every day chores."

"Yes, Jack. I'll do that. I'm sorry, but I couldn't let you get away with murder. Do you want me to take your horse to the ranch?"

"No, put her here in the livery." Janice was mad, but also weak with fright. Why had she hired such a nosey human being? "Skunk is what he is."

After Sheriff Norval locked the jail, and went home for the night, Janice cried herself to sleep. "Oh, Mama, I've failed you and Jack and Daddy. Please forgive me, but I tried to make it right. Oh God, how I tried."

That night she had a very vivid dream. A young Indian girl came and visited her in her cell. "I am Laney Hawk. I have come to guide you in your fight for life. Do not be afraid. No harm will come to you. You will not go to the town of Lincoln, tomorrow. It will be another day, if ever. Tomorrow you must send a letter to M D Thompson. He is your cousin and is a U.S. Marshal. He is at old Fort Tularosa. But even before he arrives, you will get much help.

Fear not little one, because your Spirit Guides watch over you, forever and ever. Now go to sleep and dream sweet dreams."

Janice sat up on her cot and looked all around. Not a sound was to be heard, nor anyone to see, she was alone in her dark cell. "Stupid dream!"

Chapter Six

The next morning Janice was awake early, and waiting for Sheriff Norval. She remembered her dream and knew exactly what she must do. U.S. Marshal M D Thompson, was her first cousin. Everyone called him Shorty. Janice's mother was Shorty's mother's youngest sister. Janice thought she remembered seeing him one time right after he became a U.S. Marshal. Surely he would help a relative that was in a little bit of trouble.

Sheriff Norval opened the office and went back to check on his young prisoner. "Good morning, Jack. How do you feel today? And did you sleep well last night? You know that cell bunk ain't like home."

"I'm mighty fine Sheriff, and how are you on this beautiful morning?"

"I'm fine, just fine. Why are you so happy today? Did you hear about my wife coming down with the lumbago, and I won't be able to take you over to Lincoln, today? Came on her mighty sudden like. Never before has it been this severe. It may be days before I can take you over there, unless I can get someone to stay with my wife. She wasn't even able to fix me breakfast this morning. You promise not to try and make a run for it, and I'll take you to the outhouse, then we'll go over to the cafe to eat. How does that sound?" He held the cell key up where Janice could see it, like bait.

"That's fine with me. I'm starving this morning. I didn't have supper last night, before you grabbed me and locked me up. And I give you my word, no running. But I do want to send a letter to my cousin over at old Fort Tularosa. He's a U.S. Marshal, and I'm sure he will help me out of this mess."

Sheriff Norval opened the cell door, and guided Janice out back toward the outhouse. As they walked, he said, "Well I'll be, so you have a U.S. Marshal for a cousin. And you think he'll be able to do something?"

"Yes, Sir, I do. Being as I didn't kill my folks, I'm sure he'll help me get those dirty Kraymons. Maybe he won't be as afraid of them, as you are."

Though the outhouse wall, Norval hollered, "now, boy, don't you start getting smart with me! I ain't afraid of nobody or nothing! I just do my job!" After the trip to the outhouse, they walked across the street to the small cafe and ordered breakfast. As their coffee was served, Jim walked in and sat with them. He ordered coffee and breakfast, while Janice was talking. "Good morning, Jim. Sure glad you stayed the night in town. I need you to take a letter over to old Fort Tularosa for me. It's to my cousin, Shorty. He's a U.S. Marshal. To beat that, it's a good day to start a long ride, don't you think?"

"Sure, I'll do it. But why are you so happy? You do know, you'll hang."

"Oh, I don't think so. I've got a lot of help coming, and know I won't hang for something I didn't do. So Jim, feller, look at the bright side of things, Sheriff Norval has to feed me, and even he's beginning to doubt my guilt. Look at that smile on his face."

"Now I didn't say no such thing, Jack! But being as you do have a cousin as a U.S. Marshal, well, I think you have a better chance. But, if you are guilty, he couldn't save you from hanging no matter what he is. Not from murder."

They ate breakfast, and Sheriff Norval told the cafe owner to put it on the jail's bill. Janice stood, saying, "Naw, that's all right. I'll pay for Jim's, I owe him." She frowned. "Yeah, a lot more than he thinks."

Jim mumbled out loud. "That's all right Jack. I've got to ride back out to the place and take care of the animals, before I take your letter."

"Naw, here's fifty dollars. Forty of it is your wages, and the rest is any expenses you have on the trip. I want you to push your horse pretty hard, the quicker Shorty gets here the better I'll like it. Oh, you'll need to ride on over to the Rogers' place, and have Don or Eldon take care of the animals while you're gone. It'll take at least five or six days for the round trip."

Jim headed for McCord's ranch, and Sheriff Norval took Janice back to jail. As he locked the cell door, he said, "Jack, I'll be by at noon and take you to eat. Mid-morning I'll have the Roscoe boy bring you some water. I've got to help my wife out today, that lumbago sure has her down."

Weldon Rose rode into Analla just as Butch and Roy were walking into the saloon. "Hummm, wonder what two of Sam Kraymon's boys are doing in town? Maybe a bank job. I guess I'd better go in and have myself a beer. No telling what I'll find out. Sure hope they're just traveling through."

Dismounting, Weldon tied his horse to the hitch-rail in front of the saloon. Looking around, he lifted his gun where it sat a little lighter in the holster. Walking up to the bar, he ordered a beer and looked the room over in a glance. At a table about halfway across the room sat Butch and Roy with their heads close together. With his beer in his left hand, Weldon walked back to their table. "Howdy boys, what brings y'all over this way?"

They both looked up, surprised, and Butch said, "Well howdy, Weldon. Good to see you. Sit down, sit down. We was just about to get another round. Are you ready for one?" Butch and Roy extended a hand to Weldon.

Weldon shook hands, then pulled himself a chair from the next table. "Naw, this'ns fresh. I just rode into town. What's happening in these parts that I ought'a know about?" He took a drink, and looked from one to the other.

Roy shook his head up and down to Butch, then went to get them another beer. As Weldon and Butch talked, Weldon could tell Butch was uneasy, but waited for more small talk. Butch cleared his throat and leaned forward over his empty glass. "Naw, Weldon, ain't much going on. Me and Roy thought we'd just ride over this'a way. Sure is a pretty, quiet little town, ain't it?"

Weldon looked him straight in the eyes. "Butch, why don't you quit pulling my short leg, and tell me what y'all are up to? Y'all are not thinking about robbing McFarland's bank, are you? You know, nobodies ever tried that with Sheriff Norval around. He can get nastier'n hog snot."

Butch busted out laughing. "Naw, naw. Nothing like that, honest." He looked at Weldon, and saw he wasn't satisfied with that answer. "Weldon, I'm going to tell you something. It'll raise your eye-brow, but it's on the level."

Weldon raised both eyebrows, and said, "I'm listening, Butch."

"Me and Roy's left the owl-hoot trail. We both came real close to meeting up with our maker. Kind'a made us look at life a little different. Now don't look at me that'a way, it's a fact! Anyway, this little button of a kid could have dusted both of us, but didn't. Shot me here in the leg, then asked us not to follow him anymore, or he'd kill us. And meant it to, he would'a! Norval's got him locked in jail for killing his family. Me and Roy know for a fact, he didn't do it. It was Sam and his brothers. This kid went all the way to Silver City and out gunned Ed. Billy Bonny, the lying little skunk, told us all wrong. We took up the kid's trail and he nailed five of us. Jeff was shot up real bad, so Billy took him back to town. Me and Roy went chasing this kid. Wish the heck we hadn't caught up with him. This is the littlest gun I've ever seen, but has an eye like no other. When we finally caught up to him, he let us live. Now we gotta break him out'a jail and go after the Kraymons with him. Now, Weldon, you've heard it straight."

Weldon had been watching Butch and Roy all this time. At everything Butch was saying, Roy was shaking his head up and down in adamant agreement. Weldon smiled, "I wouldn't go trying to break him out anytime soon. At least not while Sheriff Tom Norvals around. He gets all fired mighty testy about his jail and prisoners. I believe I know the kid, so why don't we team up? I'm going to help him too. But, now both of y'all know why I never ran with them Kraymons. They're a bunch of murdering sidewinders. Any man killing a woman and kid, ain't worth his salt. No matter what the reason."

For some reason, Weldon didn't ask, but Butch was clean shaven today. It was the first time Weldon had ever seen his face. He was a lot younger than anyone would have thought. Weldon thought to himself, "Heck, he's just a kid hisself. No more than thirty. Maybe even less than that."

"What do you think you can do that me and Roy can't?" Butch grinned.

"First off, I ain't never been in trouble with no law. And I've knowed Norval for nigh on to fifteen years. Long enough to call him a friend. I can talk to him and see what he's got on young Jack, and what he's going to do."

Roy was stuttering and shaking his head, as he asked, "What did you mean, you ain't never been in trouble with no law?"

"Just because I hang around with you boys, and the like, that don't mean I'm an outlaw. I'm just your little above average gambler and had to get good with my gun to stay alive, that's all. You've never heard of me being in on a job, or in trouble with the law. Now let's find out where that kid lives and ride out to his place. I'd like to get the feeling of where the kid lives.

Just maybe we can find something Norval didn't. Anyway, we've got to figure out what we can do, legal like." Weldon downed his beer, and headed for the door, with a determined look about him.

Weldon was thinking as he got his horse from the hitch rail, then walked with Butch and Roy to the livery. They saddled their horses and rode down the street. Sheriff Norval left the mercantile and was walking across the street toward his home. Stopping to let the horses pass, he looked up at Weldon. "Well, howdy, Weldon. Riding through?" He held out his hand.

"Howdy, Tom. Naw, I'll be hanging around for a spell. I've got a little business here abouts." Taking Norval's hand in a shake, he nodded toward Butch and Roy. "Oh, this here is Butch and Roy. They'll be riding along with me for awhile. Say, I hear'd you went and locked up that kid, Jack McCord. Locked him up for something

I can't believe he did. Killing his parents, that right? Is that what you got him charged with?"

"Yeah. I was going to take him over to Lincoln today, but my wife came down with the lumbago. Sure was strange, just overnight she came down. Why are you interested in that McCord kid?" He looked at each man.

"He didn't do the killing. It was the Kraymons. Me and these two boys are going to prove it." Weldon watched the surprised look on Tom's face.

"I don't know, Weldon, we'll see. Well, I gotta get this medicine home. Guess I'll see y'all around. I think yer beat'n a dead horse, he's guilty."

Weldon, Butch and Roy rode out in a gallop. About half way to the McCord place, they met Jim. He was on his way to old Fort Tularosa to give Shorty Thompson, Jack's letter. They all jerked to a stop in a cloud of dust, as Butch pulled his gun on Jim. Everyone was surprised, including Jim.

Weldon shouted, "What in the heck are you doing, Butch?"

"This here is the little skunk what grabbed Jack's gun and got him arrested. I think I'll make it right. Maybe put a couple of big ol' holes in him and let him think about what he went and done."

Jim sat with his eyes narrowed. At first he thought they were robbers holding him up. When he heard what Butch had to say, he blurted out, "Hey, at the time, I didn't know but what Jack was the one that did the killings. I work for him, and while he was gone, I found the graves covered up with a pile of hay. What was I suppose to think? Anyway, he's got a cousin over at old Fort Tularosa that's a U.S. Marshal. I'm on my way over there now to get him. It'll take me a good five or six days to make the round trip."

All three men were giving him the evil eye, and didn't believe a word he had said. Jim saw he wasn't getting anywhere. "Look, if you don't believe me, here's Jack's letter. I'm taking it to his cousin." Sweat formed on a lip.

Butch reached out and jerked it from his hand. "He's telling it true. This letter is addressed to U.S. Marshal M D Thompson, Fort Tularosa, New Mexico Territory. Who's watching the livestock while you're gone?"

"Nobody. I tried to get the Rogers, but they were busy, so I turned everything out in the pasture. They'll have grass to eat, and plenty of water to drink until I get back."

Weldon leaned forward in his saddle, saying, "we'll be staying there some. We're personal friends of Jack's, and are figuring a way to help him. Don't worry about the stock, we'll take care of everything while you're gone."

Jim sat a little straighter in the saddle. "Well now, I don't know about strangers staying around a place with nobody else about."

Butch looked him in the eyes. "Why you little snot! We didn't ask, we said we was staying, and that's that! You're the one that helped put him in jail, we're getting him out! Now you'd best ride your rump off, and get that letter delivered. If we're not here when you get back, don't worry about it, we'll be around later." They watched after Jim until he rode from sight in a cloud of dust, glancing back at them over his shoulder.

Half an hour later they rode into McCord's yard. Weldon looked around, "Man, it's a crying shame how a bunch of low lifes can take a man and his family away from a place like this. You can tell they had poured their hearts into making something out of it. Wonder how big'a place it is, noway?"

Butch and Roy had stepped from their horses and were looking everything over. Throwing his saddle over a fence rail, Butch said, "I saw the Whip Cord brand on everything for the last five miles or so. Must be fair sized. Let's put these horses away, and see what we can do. Everything looks to be a hell of a mess."

Over the next three days the men had discovered an irrigation system for the fields. The water gate was about a half mile up stream, and they had the fields flooded in no time at all. It had been years since any of the three men had had a shovel in their hands, but they cleaned the water ditches and watered the fields. They worked from sunup until just before dark, then Roy would go to the house and cook supper while Butch and Weldon took care of the evening chores.

Talking after supper, the decision was made to just ride in and get Jack out of jail, one way or another. Then they all would go looking for the Kraymons. Both Roy and Butch thought that was a heck of an idea. Weldon was serious when he said, "Now look, both of you. Y'all let me do the talking, I've known Tom for years. We'll take care of the livestock first thing in the morning, then we'll all ride in." Weldon had some doubts .

Sheriff Norval wasn't in his office, and the front door was locked. Butch said he'd be glad to shoot it off, but Weldon thought that might be a bad idea.

Roy suggested going across the street for a beer, and inquire of the where abouts of the Sheriff. "He might already took Jack to Lincoln. I sure hope not though. It'd be a lot easier taking Jack from Norval, than Garrett. Them deputies of Garrett's are about as crazy as any I've seen." Then shook his head up and down in agreement to what he had said.

Butch rolled a smoke, and asked Weldon, "What do you think about it? Think he's already gone?"

"Let's go around to a window and holler. Maybe Jack will answer. Roy, you wait out front here, just in case Tom comes back." Weldon and Butch walked around beside the building and to the only window.

"Hey, Jack, you in there?" They waited a couple of minutes.

Janice climbed on her bunk and grabbed on to the bars. With her face pressed close to the bars, she hollered, "Weldon! What are you doing here? I thought I heard Butch and Roy's voice's out front. You know, they followed me and tried to kill me! You watch them two, good. They're sneaky!"

Butch laughed, "yeah Jack, that was before I knowed you. Roy's around front waiting on Norval. We're going to bust you out of there."

"Butch, it that you, with no beard??"

"Yep, it's me. Good lookin', huh? Where's the Sheriff this morning?"

"He'll be here around ten o'clock, he's taking me over to Lincoln today. He said I'd be in jail over there for better'n a month before the Circuit Judge showed up. I sure hope my cousin Shorty, can help, I'm really in a pickle."

Before Weldon could say a word, Butch blurted out, "Don't you worry none, Jack. We're going to have you out of there by ten- fifteen at the latest. You just hold on a bit longer, we'll be right back."

They walked around front, and sat on the jail steps until Sheriff Norval walked up. "Howdy, boys. Something I can do for you fellers?"

They all three stood, and Weldon asked, "how long have we knowed each other, Tom? And been friends?" He stood square in front of the sheriff.

"I'd guess nigh on to fifteen years, why?" Norval had a puzzled look.

"Have you ever knowed of me lying to any man, or going back on my word for anything?" Weldon watched Tom's face, and waited for an answer.

"Naw, never nothing like that. Say, what's going on here, noway?" "Jack   said it'd be a little over a month before the judge got to Lincoln. Is that about right?" Weldon was still watching the Sheriff's face.

"Yeah, give or take a few days. Why are y'all interested in the judge?"

Butch blurted out, "'cause we're gonna take..."

Before he could say anymore, Weldon cut in, giving Butch the wicked eye, which told him to shut his mouth. "Tom, I want you to release Jack to me. We'll have him in front of that judge when the time comes, and won't be late. Meantime, we're going to get the Kraymons, and prove that Jack had nothing to do with killing his family."

"Weldon, you know I can't do a thing like that! What if he makes a run for it? Why, I might never find him again." Tom was shocked at the thought.

"Did you go hunting him the first time, or did he just walk into your office?" Butch was standing with his hands on his hips, glaring at Tom.

"Well, yeah, he walked in. But he didn't know that I knew about his folks. Hadn't been for that young feller he hired, we probably wouldn't know it now. He'd done a good job of covering those graves."

Butch saw they weren't getting anywhere with Sheriff Norval. Roy was standing over to the side with his hand only inches above his gun butt. He had been shaking his head either from side to side or up and down. Butch looked Tom in the eye. "You mean you've knowed Weldon darn near forever, and his word don't mean dittly squat to you! I'll tell you what, Norval, either Jack goes with us now, and we have him in Lincoln on time, or I gut shoot you right here and now, and we take him! Now you answer me! What do you think of that? You hard-headed, no good sack of rotten...!" Butch was steaming mad.

Weldon cut in one more time. "Tom, I won't take him by force, but if you don't let him go with us, mine and your friendship ends right here and now. Him going with us is the only way we can clear him. His Marshal cousin should be on his way right now. You can tell him which way we headed. We're going to White Oaks, then over to Fort Sumner. We'll be able to pick up a trail somewhere north or west of here. We've got to try, Jack has no other chance, so what do you say?" Weldon had never ask another man for nothing.

Tom eyed all three men. Never had he looked into harder eyes in his life. "All right, Weldon! But you're right, our friendship rides on you having Jack in Lincoln by the time the Circuit Judge shows up. My job could be at stake, and y'all's lives. And Butch, don't ever threaten me again, or you'll have to eat that gun! Now let's go in and get Jack."

Chapter Seven

Shorty read the letter from Jack, and turned to his ranch partner. "Buffalo, looks like I've got a problem over in the Rio Hondo Valley. This letter is from my little fifteen year old cousin. He says five men came in and gunned down his family, and now the Sheriff has him locked up for the murders. He's my dead mother's, sister's boy. I'll be riding out in the morning with Jim. I don't know how long I'll be gone, but you have everything ready, and when I get back, and we'll head up to Wyoming for some more of your gold."

"Think I ought'a come with you now?" Buffalo had a sad look.

"Naw, Buffalo, you know this is early August, and falls coming on, then winter will be here before you can blow your nose twice. If you go with me now, we couldn't head to Wyoming until next spring. Whatever's all right."

Buffalo looked rejected, but said, "You think you can handle it alone?"

"Yeah, I shouldn't have much trouble. I'll be back in a few weeks at the most. I'll get Pat Garrett, if I need any help. He knows that country."

The next morning Shorty saddled his dun stud and had his bedroll and rain slicker. Buffalo asked him why he didn't take a pack horse along. "Cause I'm gonna be traveling hard and fast. I want to get who ever done it, and get on back. Don't look so worried, Buffalo. I'll be all right. Don't act like an old mother hen. You're acting like a slapped around kid."

Two nights later Shorty and Jim spent the night in Kelly. Jim had never been in a silver mining boom town before, and sure liked the ladies that worked in the saloons. Shorty got to visit with Jobe Enoch, an old friend of his. Since Dunhill and his crooked bunch were no longer around, Kelly had quieted down to a slow roar. Card sharks and con men by the dozens still worked the miners, but that was to be expected.

Two more days of hard riding, and they rode into Analla. It was late evening, so they ate supper, then got a hotel room. They would talk with Sheriff Norval come morning.

Shorty and Jim had just finished with breakfast when Sheriff Norval walked into the cafe for coffee. Seeing Jim and Shorty, he walked over to their table. "Howdy, Jim. Took a bit longer than you thought it would, going to Fort Tularosa and back."

"Yes, Sir. It's a hard ride. This here's U.S. Marshal, M D Thompson, Jack's cousin. But you knowed that, didn't you?"

"Yes, Jim, I knew that." Sticking out his hand to Shorty, he said, "Howdy, Marshal. I'm Tom Norval, the local Sheriff here abouts."

Shorty stood, shaking his hand. "Howdy, Tom. Sit for some coffee. Think you can tell me something about the McCord killings?"

"Yeah, but I imagine Jim has told you as much as I know. Jack hired him to take care of the livestock while he rode off somewhere. Anyway a couple of days after he was gone, the cattle broke down a fence and got into some hay. That's when Jim here found the grave markers. He said was hid real good. Then he came and told me about it, and a week later Jack walked into my office. I arrested him and was going to take him over to Lincoln for the Circuit Judge. Before I could do that, three men came and I released Jack to them. They're going to have him in Lincoln by the time the Judge gets there."

"Why in the world would you release a prisoner to three men? Were they lawmen?" Shorty took a sip of coffee, and watched Tom's face.

Tom blushed and stammered just a might, saying, "Naw, naw, they're anything but lawmen. Although, I have known one of them for nigh on to fifteen years. He is a man of his word. He said he'd have Jack in Lincoln, and he'll by darned have Jack in Lincoln. I've staked my reputation and job on it."

Shorty would have laughed, if this hadn't been so serious. He sat, and pushed his hat all the way back on his head. "Where are these three men now? And when will the judge be in Lincoln? Didn't Jack believe I'd come?" Shorty was full of questions, and they all came out at once.

"Yes, he knew you'd come, but they went on after the Kraymons. They're the ones that Jack said killed his family. Two of the men are, or were Kraymon men, until Jack went to Silver City and out gunned Ed Kraymon. He also shot one of these in the leg, then they followed him back here so they could help him get the Kraymons. Now dang-it, don't look at me that way! I know it's crazy, but every bit of it's true! They was going to take Jack whether I let them or not. That man called Butch, said he'd gut shoot me to get Jack out. I don't think Weldon would have let it go that far, but they are gone. Before they left, Weldon said for me to tell you that they were heading for White Oaks and then to Fort Sumner. This whole thing's a mess, huh?"

Shorty had sat and listened to something that was hard to understand. "This man, Weldon, would his last name happen to be Rose?"

"Yeah, that's him. Have you heard of him?" Tom's face brightened.

"Yeah, I've heard a good deal about him. And you're right, he is honest. Can you believe it, an honest gambler? I'd say one in a million, or there abouts. Oh, one other thing, you said something about grave markers."

"Yeah, huge suckers. Jack made 'em hisself and put 'em on the graves. I've never seen 'em though. Jim has." Tom held his hand about waist high.

"And you still think a mad dog killer would take time to do that?"

"You know, Marshal, I've been thinking somewhat about that. Why don't we just ride out to the McCord place, and take ourselves a look. Maybe we can find something that was over looked."

"Yeah, that's what I thought I'd do. But how do you suppose Jack, a kid, got good enough to out gun Ed Kraymon? And Jim needs to get out to the ranch and take care of the animals. Ain't that right, Jim?"

"Yeah, it is. But I wonder what kind of shape it'll be in after them three fellers stayed awhile. Probably one heck of a mess."

The same morning Shorty and Jim had left Kelly, was the morning Sheriff Norval let Jack go with Weldon, Butch and Roy. After getting Jack's horse from the livery, they headed east toward the McCord Ranch. Janice was surprised at how good looking Butch was without the beard. And Roy looked the same, pudgy, jolly and still shaking his head up and down. Janice wondered how and why he ever became an outlaw.

Janice had been gone from home nigh on to two weeks, and could hardly believe her eyes. The fields had been watered and the crops sure looked good. "Boy, that Jim sure knows how to farm. Would you just look at this place. Everything is cleaned up, and well, I couldn't have done better."

Butch arched an eye-brow and looked at Janice. "Jack, boy, it wadn't Jim what did all of this work. It was Weldon, and Roy, and me. We worked our rumps off for three days out here. All we did was repair fences, and clear weeds from them water ditches. They hadn't been cleaned at all. Water wouldn't have run down 'em if we hadn't cleaned 'em. We done it! Not that little snot! Grabbing your gun that'a way, I ought'a shot him!"

"Naw, you didn't shoot him, did you? But thanks, to all three of you. If y'all will put the horses away, I'll see if there's any food left, and start dinner. I won't be heading out after the Kraymons until sometime tomorrow."

Janice walked inside the house, and the men took the horses. Weldon started unsaddling his and Janice's horses. "Butch, Roy, we got us a touchy situation here. I don't think Jack is expecting us to go along after Sam and the boys. When we sit down to dinner, I'm going to do some talking. Y'all listen and don't say a word until I'm done. You can sit with your mouths open, just don't let nothing come out. Butch, are you listening to me?" Weldon glared at him with one eye. "Butch?"

"Yeah, yeah, I heard you. I'll keep my mouth shut, but I'm going whether the kid wants me to or not. We don't know how many men Sam's got riding with him right now. Prod'ly be more'n Jack can handle."

All Roy did was shake his head up and down, or from side to side, it was according to how the conversation was going. Weldon eyed them both. "Butch, we're all going. I just have to talk Jack into it, and believe me, it's going to be a shock to both of you, and Jack." He snickered to himself.

After the horses were watered and fed, they sat on the porch talking and waiting for dinner to get ready. An hour later Janice walked out and said, "Y'all can wash up, it'll be ready by then. It's not much, but we'll have a better supper. I've got beans soaking and a salted ham roast in the oven."

They all walked in and sat down as Janice poured coffee for everyone except herself, she drank water.

With his mouth about half full, Butch asked, "Jack, my boy, how in the world did you ever learn to cook like this? Man, this is good grub."

"Oh, my mama showed me how when I was just a little kid. She said I'd never know when it'd come in handy. And it already has."

When finished with their meal, they kicked back and drank more coffee. Weldon was sitting across the table from Janice. He leaned back his chair on two legs and cleared his throat. "Yes, Sir, Janice, you're a darn good cook. Best meal I've had in a long, long time." He smiled right big.

"Why thank you Wel..., what do you mean, 'Janice'?" She turned pale and started her chair backward. Fright was in her eyes.

Weldon took another sip of coffee, while Roy and Butch froze with their cups at their lips, eyes going from Weldon to Janice and back again. "Janice, I've know'd you wasn't Jack all along. I let it go this long because that's the way you wanted it. But now, you're going up against some old boys that will chew you up and spit you out. Butch and Roy both have rode with the Kraymons. I haven't, but I've knowed 'em a good while. Like Sam, for instance, he carries a hide-out in his boot, and if in a bind, he'll give hisself up until he gets a chance to pull that hide-out gun. He'll kill you and spit on your body and kick you in the head at the same time."

Janice sat with a surprised, but angry look on her face. "Well, Mr. know it all, smarty pants! Just how did you find out I was Janice? And if y'all think you're telling another living soul, you're badly mistaken!"

"Now hold your horses. I'm not telling anybody else. I'm here to help you, just like Butch and Roy are. Do you remember when we got to the Rio Grande, and it was so dad-gummed hot, and you wouldn't go swimming? Boys always go swimming, excuse or not. Then I went and killed that rabbit for our supper." Weldon was watching Janice's face.

"Yes, I remember all of that, what does that have to do with anything?"

"Look at my hands, and pay close attention to my little fingers." Everyone watched as Weldon brought his hands to his mouth as if he were eating a piece of rabbit. The little fingers on both hands were held up and away from his mouth.

Janice jumped to her feet. "My God! I do that, don't I?"

"Yes, Missy, you do. Now, me and the boys here don't mind you being a girl, and we won't tell nobody until you do. Myself, I'm mighty proud of you for what you have done, and still trying to do. But you have to be man, or as it is, woman enough to accept help when it's offered in good faith." Weldon watched her face.

Janice slowly sat down with her hands folded in her lap. She looked from one face to another. "Butch, Roy, I'm sorry, but I had to do everything I did. And I'm really glad you're not mad at me anymore, and that you're on my side. Also I'm glad I didn't kill you two back there on the trail." She giggled.

Butch smiled. "Don't you worry yourself about it. We all know why you did it. As Janice, you would have gotten nowhere. But as Jack, and learning how to use those guns, well, I'd have never knowed you was a girl. Just leave it up to a gambler who watches faces and hands. Boy, you're good, Weldon, dad-gummed good. Don't you think so, Roy?" Roy's head had been totally still during the whole conversation.

"Yep, sure do. But I just can't get over Jack being a Janice. How can a young girl do what she's done? Dang it all mighty, very few growed men could have took Ed, much less a kid, and a girl at that!" Roy shook his head again, up and down in agreement with himself.

Janice had composed herself, and said, "I'm glad y'all don't hold nothing against me, because I'm still going after the Kraymons. But how will y'all feel, riding with a girl?" She gave her crooked little smiled.

Roy laughed out loud. "Pretty darn safe's how I'll feel. You're better'n most when it comes to them guns." He shook his head up and down, and laughed out loud.

Janice looked across the table at Weldon. "Weldon, you seem to have something on your mind, and you're not ready to talk about it. If y'all are in this with me, I think you'd better lay it all on the table, now. And don't come up with the idea that I ain't going along, because I am, no matter what you come up with." Her eyes were glaring.

"Naw, nothing like that. It's just going to be mighty strange calling you Jack, when we all know you're a Janice."

"All y'all have to remember is, Janice is dead until this is all over. That's why I put my name on Jack's grave. So everyone would think it was me in there. And it'll stay there until this is over."

Weldon looked at her, saying, "you did the right thing. Sure was mighty smart of you to figure this all out. Most men couldn't have done it."

Butch added, "yeah, for a fact, I couldn't have done what you have."

The next morning they put a little traveling grub in their saddle bags and headed for White Oaks. Leaving the Rio Hondo Valley, their horses climbed steep mountains going northwest. By the middle of the afternoon, they rode into a narrow valley and were riding down White Oak's main street.

"Jack, we'd better stop off at the saloon and find out if any of Sam's boys have been around lately. No telling how long it'll take. Do you want to hang around outside, or do something else for awhile?" Weldon was watching Janice's face for a reaction, and got one.

"No, that's all right, I'll go in with you. I've been in a stinking, gut wagon saloon before. Matter of fact, I killed Ed in one over in Silver City." Janice smiled, "Its a good place to kill a dog, in a hog pen."

Butch turned sideways in his saddle to look at her. "Well, don't go getting us into trouble in here. After all, I know most of the men that come in this saloon." Butch was serious. "Some are still my friends, at least I hope they are. I don't want you killing them all."

As they dismounted, Janice said, "If they leave me alone, they'll be safe." She laughed out loud, and then giggled.

The three men ordered beer, and got Janice a sarsaparilla. Weldon motioned to a table, and headed that way. One of the ladies of the saloon caught Janice by the arm, and said, "I like 'em young, cowboy. How about a little tussling roll in the hay?" She purred, "I'll make it special, just for you."

Janice jerked free, hollering, "take your cotton-picking hands off me, lady! I don't roll in the hay with nobody!" She was red faced and mad.

Butch hollered back over his shoulder, "Jack, dad-gum-it! Let that woman go, and get on over here! You're holding up our card game."

Even Roy had to snicker at that, while he shook his head up and down.

"Me! Let her go!" Janice grabbed her sarsaparilla and took a chair facing the smiling woman. She looked from Butch to Weldon. "Are all the women in saloons as brazen as that one? I thought I was going to have to pistol whip her just to get loose. Man, but she's got a grip."

"Naw, they're not all like that, some are worse. Most would have had you in their room and money out of your pocket before they even started talking. That kind can smell money, and probably thought your rich daddy sent you in here for some..., uh, well, uh, to get acquainted with the ladies." Butch grinned, then laughed out loud.

Every time Janice looked her way, the woman would make eyes at her. She finally had enough and said, "Look, are we going to find the Kraymons, or are y'all going to sit around playing cards all day? That woman is driving me crazy! If she makes eyes at me one more time... I'll, I'll gut shoot her!"

"Jack, this is the middle of the afternoon! Most men don't start filling a saloon until after dark. Why don't you go over and get yourself a room. If any of the Kraymons come in, one of us will come and get you before anything happens. But no matter, one of the boys that come in here will know where they've gone. If they're not here, we'll follow them come morning."

Janice looked Weldon in the eye. "Now Weldon, you're not pulling my leg, are you? Y'all will come and get me?"

With exasperation in his voice, Weldon said, "Jack, this is your deal all the way. We're just here to keep everybody off your back. Remember Ed? If Billy had thought you could take Ed, he'd been on your back. Now go on and get yourself something to eat, and a hotel room. We'll stay here all night anyway. And we may have ourselves a long hard ride starting tomorrow. You had better get all the rest you can, while you can."

As Janice walked out the door, Butch got up and started asking around about the Kraymons. He found that Sam had been in White Oaks a little over a week ago, waiting for Ed. When the Bristol gang showed up, they all left together for the Santa Fe Trail. They were going to hold up travelers and stage coaches for awhile. It was getting to hazardous to rob mine payrolls in this area, with all the extra guards on every run.

The man that was telling Butch this, had been shot in the arm on his last job. He knew Butch and Roy had worked with Sam, and just figured they were looking for a job or two. Before Butch went back to Roy and Weldon, he bought the man a beer and said, "Thanks, Buster. I'll tell Sam you're feeling better and will join up when you can."

Back at the table, Butch told Weldon everything. Weldon rubbed his full beard, thinking out loud. "Dad-gum-it! That's a long way for Jack to ride. You boys do know we'll have to start all the way over to Las Vegas. No telling how much farther we'll ride after that. That would be my best bet being as it's on the Santa Fe Trail. If Las Vegas is where they're holed up, they hit the stage and anything else between there and Santa Fe. Otherwise, they'd have to go darn near to Raton, and maybe east. That's just too danged far, naw, it's gotta be Las Vegas. Fort Union is a third of the way to Raton, and Sam wouldn't chance robbing too close to there. We'll tell Jack about it in the morning. Who knows, maybe she'll, I mean he'll want to wait until they all get back here." Looking the other two men in the face, he laughed out loud. "In a big fat pig's rump, huh?" He laughed again and dealt the cards.

They were eating breakfast when Janice walked in, as mad as a wet hen about all the wasted time. They should have been fifty miles further down the road instead of them sitting around drinking and playing cards. "Remember, we don't have all that much time! You've got to have me in Lincoln by the first of the month." Looking around the table, her eyes stopped on Weldon.

"Jack, just stay calm. Don't pop a cork. We've got all the time we'll need. Butch found out exactly what we need to know. It'll take a day and a half for us to get to Las Vegas, then tomorrow night we'll find out which side of town the robberies are taking place. Could you have done better? No, I think not. You'd have gunned down the first man who said he even knew the Kraymons. Jack, we can't get in too much of a hurry. You don't want one of us to getting killed, do you?" He stared her in the eyes.

"No, no, of course not! I'm just too dad-gummed impatient for my own good. I know y'all are doing the best that can be done. So, let's ride."

"Jack! We're going to finish breakfast and have a couple more cups of coffee! My God, it's not as if they was going to up and leave the country. They're around and we'll find them. Now sit down and eat." Weldon's look made Janice realize she couldn't get in too much of a hurry with these three along. If they keep slowing her down, well she may have to go on alone. She would just sneak off and...

An hour later they were in a long lope, headed for Las Vegas. By pushing their horses fast, they could spend the night in Anton Chico. That would be better than somewhere out on the trail, and there was a cafe and saloon, besides the hotel. The hotel was small, and had only nine rooms, but this wasn't a weekend or the first of the month. They'd get rooms, no problem, and tomorrow, barring any trouble, they could make it to Las Vegas by mid-afternoon. The Kraymons were somewhere close, Weldon could smell them.

As Janice and her three body guards, as they had come to call each other, rode from Fort Sumner, Shorty, Jim, and Sheriff Norval were riding to the McCord Ranch. When they were three quarters of a mile from the house, Jim looked down toward the Rio Hondo River, and at the fields along its banks. Shorty watched as Jim stood in the stirrups and looked back up stream, then turned his head down river.

"What's up, Jim? Something wrong that me and Tom ought'a know about?" Shorty was concerned.

"Well, yeah. I mean, no. It's just that that fence along the river has been repaired, and all the water ditches have been cleaned of weeds, and the fields have all been watered. Heck fire, I ain't been gone a week and I'd swear that corn has growed a foot. I knowed it needed watering before I left, but I didn't have time to do everything. I had hoped it would rain, but it didn't, I don't guess. Oh, I know, the Rogers boys came over after all and done it. They knowed Jack needed the help. Yeah, that's what happened."

As they rode into the yard, Jim got another surprise. All the weeds along the porch and around the house had been pulled, and were piled off to one side. "Boy, them Rogers boys sure know how to take care of a place.

Now, believe me, I would have pulled all them weeds, and cleaned this place up, I just hadn't had the time. I reckon that's all I'll have now though, is time."

Jim dismounted in front of the house, but Shorty and Sheriff Norval rode on down to the orchard. They got off their horses and dropped the reins. The fence had been repaired, and the hay was gone. Tom guessed someone took it to the barn. Shorty opened the small gate, and stood looking at the graves. Removing his hat, he read the markers aloud. "This is hard to believe."

"It must'a took days to make these markers. Good job, huh, Shorty?"

"Yeah, I'd bet so. I can see it wasn't Jack that did the killings. Too much love went into making those markers. Why didn't you ever come out here and look the murder sight over? If you'd seen this, surely you'd listened to Jack. Like I've already said, it wasn't Jack. Maybe he saw that it was the Kraymons when they did the killings."

"Yeah, lot'a things I ought'a done different." Norval hung his head. "You know, Shorty, I sure feel bad about the way I've handled things."

"Yeah, I can understand that. Do you have any idea where the Kraymons might be now? I need to get after Jack and those men."

"Naw, but Butch and Roy have rode with them and the Bristol gang. If anybody can find them, those two can. They told me they was going to start looking at White Oaks, then maybe all the way over to Fort Sumner."

"By the way, didn't you say that Jack also shot and killed Ed Kraymon?" Shorty asked this, wondering if he had heard right.

"Yeah, that's what Butch and Roy told me. Jack out-draw'd Ed flat out."

"Now how in the world did this fifteen year old boy get so dad-gummed good with a hand gun? Ed just must have been extra slow."

"I have no idea, but that ain't all. Jack out-gunned two of the Bristol gang right here at the barn. They rode in here after robbing the bank over at White Oaks, and was going to ride off on two of the McCord horses. Jack shot 'em both dead, and one of them already had his gun in his hand."

Shorty closed the gate, and they rode back to the house. Jim heard them and came outside. "Well, find anything that will help? He stood bare-headed, and felt naked. "Just a minute, I'll get my hat."

"That's all right, we're leaving. If Jack comes back, tell him I'm looking for the Kraymons. Tell him he ought'a hang around here until I get back."

"Yeah, sure, I'll tell him, for all the good it'll do. Y'all ride easy."

Shorty and Tom talked very little while riding back to Analla. Shorty wondered why Tom, or even Pat Garrett wasn't out trying to round up the Kraymons. Someone should have at least had a doubt about Jacks guilt. "If Jack is after the Kraymons, he must have seen the killings, and knows exactly who did it. Tom, how dependable are Butch and Roy? From what I've heard about Weldon, he'll ride the line for Jack. I just don't know the other two. And how did Jack talk them into helping him?"

"I figger they'll go all the way. Heck fire, Butch wanted to gut shoot me just to get Jack out'a jail! I certainly don't pose the threat to Jack that them Kraymons do. By now they've got to know it was Jack that killed Ed."

"Yeah, I suppose you're right. I'll stay the night in Analla, then get on their trail right after breakfast. Let's kick these horses out a bit."

As they rode up main street, four men backed from the bank with their guns in their hands. In the street stood one man holding five horses. Tom glanced at Shorty and exclaimed, "Would you look at that? A bank robbery in my town! Give me a hand, Shorty. Let's put a stop to this right now!"

Shorty and Tom drew their guns just as the men turned to mount their horses. One of them shouted, "It's the Sheriff! Lets ride!" He was the only one to get off a shot. He and the other three that had exited the bank were laying dead in the street. The horse holder dropped the reins and held his hands high. "I didn't know what they was doing, Marshal! Honest! I was just told to hold these horses!"

Mr. McFarland came running from the bank, and picked up the fallen bags of money. Looking over his spectacles, he shouted, "Tom! Thank the Lord you're here! Those men would have gotten away with the contents of one of my vaults! They never saw the other two that were facing my desk. Lordy, Lordy, what would the county have done?" Mr. McFarland looked relieved.

"Wellll, I'm just mighty glad me and Shorty rode up at the right time.

Oh, Mr. McFarland, this is U.S. Marshal Shorty Thompson. He's over here to see if he can help out Jack McCord. It's looking mighty strong now that Jack didn't kill his folks. Maybe the Kraymons did it after all. At least that's what Shorty thinks." He gave a quick glance at Shorty.

Mr. McFarland shook hands with Shorty and smiled. "Shorty Thompson. You wouldn't happen to be kin to a Shorty Thompson I knew down in Wellington, Texas, fifteen or so years ago, would you? You look a lot alike."

"Yes, Sir, that was my father. He died when I was eleven, so that was fourteen years ago. But I do remember you. You owned a bank there also."

"Yes, yes, that's true. I certainly did. Well, I see I'm keeping you men from hanging this fellow. Marshal Thompson, stop by my house for supper."

"Thank you, Sir. I might just do that."

Tom removed the robbers gun, while Shorty removed the dead men's guns and looked for papers. Then they walked a frightened man to jail. Shorty dropped the dun's reins over the hitch rail and tied Tom's horse. Walking inside, he dropped all the guns on Tom's desk. He snickered to himself when he saw Tom standing by the open cell, listening to a sobbing man try to make a deal. 'Listen, Sheriff, you've got it all wrong. If you'll just drop the robbery charges against me, I've got a lot I can tell you about the Kraymons." He saw the Sheriff raise an eyebrow. "And the Bristols too! They're the ones you want, not me. You let me go and I'll leave this territory and never, ever come back. Now that's a solemn oath, never!"

Tom shoved him inside the cell and locked the door. Turning to Shorty, he winked and put the outlaw's gun in a desk drawer.

"Now ain't that just like an outlaw, Shorty. You luck out and get the gang leader, and he can't wait to sell out his whole gang. At least the ones that are still alive. But..., this one will hang come Monday. Yeah, Mondays are always a good day for a hanging. Man, I just love Monday hangings!"

Shorty laughed out loud. "Boy you got that right. Start your week off with a good hanging, and your whole week goes better. Yes, sir, it does."

The outlaw was hollering in a high-pitched whine. "Naw, naw, dang-it Sheriff, I ain't the boss! You can't hang me for that bank robbery! We didn't get away with no money. We didn't even kill nobody. Please, Sheriff, you gotta listen to me! Ohhh, please, please listen! Come on Sheriff, you gotta."

"All right, you have my word as Sheriff, you won't hang. I'll talk with the judge and see you get no more than a few years. Now, what you have to tell me had better be good, or all bets are off. And another thing, I find that you're lying, I'll hang you before you see a judge! Now say what all do you have to say? And, I'll be looking you in the eye. You lie to me and..."

"It was the Kraymons, and that's the truth. Sam and his brothers came over here a couple of months back, and looked the town over. While they was here, Henry McCord whipped up on Sam pretty good fer kissin' his wife. And a couple days later him and his brothers went out to the McCord place, and raped the misses and killed 'em all. But we guess the boy lived, 'cause he went and killed Ed over at Silver City. Anyway they went up north along the Santa Fe Trail, and told us to come down here and hit this bank. I was told to hold the horses, that's all. Said nobody was around, and not to worry about the Sheriff none. Guess he was wrong, huh?" He sadly flopped down on the cot, with his face in his hands.

Tom was leaning against the wall, across from the cell. "Yep, you sure got that right. I'm just glad Shorty was along when y'all tried it. Wasn't for him, I'd probably be totin' lead. What's your name, young feller?"

"Casper, Casper Wiggins. Yer not really going to hang me, are you Sheriff? I told it straight and true, and I was just holding the horses, honest!"

"Naw, Casper, I'm not going to hang you. I'll take you over to the county seat in a day or two. I'll turn you over to Garrett, but I'll talk with the judge and let him know how you helped me clear a young boy of some murders he didn't do. It looks like Jack was right all along, the Kraymons did it. You just settle back awhile, and I'll bring you some supper after a bit."

Shorty smiled, "Well Tom, it looks like you could have been an actor. Your scare tactics sure did work, and that little feller talked his guts out. I guess with all that's been said, Jack won't have to be in Lincoln after all."

"Naw, he won't have to be there. But I sure do have to eat crow. And dad-gum-it, I should'a knowed Jack didn't kill his family! Shucks fire, I've know'd him since he was a baby. Always a nice kid; worked real hard and was forever helping out folks in need. The whole family came in to church as often as they could. And you know, Shorty, McFarland told me that kid is pretty dang rich now that his folks are dead. Now that I look at it, if he'd killed his folks, he'd grabbed that money from the bank and hit the trail. I'd never caught him. But naw, he didn't do that, he just went after the killers. Darn my sorry hide, I should'a thought things out a little better. Well, when he gets back, I'll shake his hand and tell him how sorry I am. And be glad to do it."

Shorty stood and said, "I'd better get some sleep, and get me an early start in the morning. I need to find Jack and those fellers he's riding with before they do something they ought'n. Or maybe get into something they can't get out of."

Chapter Eight

Shorty was on the trail before sunup. If he made good time, he could be in White Oaks shortly after noon. He thought to himself how he needed to get this job over with pronto. He and Buffalo were wanting to get up to Wyoming and pick up another load of gold. Shorty had never been to where Buffalo had found all that gold, but the four hundred pounds he had brought out was almost pure. They had bought their ranch with some of it.

Remembering all of this, Shorty patted the dun on the neck and said, "Ain't a bad deal, huh Dunnie. Me a U.S. Marshal and a rich rancher too boot. Keeps you fed, huh?"

The first person Shorty saw in White Oaks was Pat Garrett. Stopping the dun beside Pat, he lowered his hand for a shake. "Howdy, Pat."

"Howdy, Shorty. I'm busier than a cat in a rock pile. Heard about Jack.

It's too hard for me to believe that kid did such a thing. He's too outstanding."

"Yeah, that's why I'm over this away. He didn't kill his folks, it was Sam

Kraymon's bunch. Sheriff Norval and me had us a bank robber that talked his head off. Tom will be taking him over to your jail in a few days. I'm looking for Jack and the three men who are riding with him. They have taken it upon themselves to go after the Kraymons. It's Weldon Rose, Butch and Roy. You haven't seen them, have you? I was told they headed this way."

"Naw, I ain't seen 'em. But they was by here a couple of days ago. Smitty Koonz said they headed toward Las Vegas. Say, Shorty, why don't you get yourself a room, then meet me in the saloon for a drink or two? I've got to stay the night here, and take a prisoner back to Lincoln, tomorrow. Then I've got to ride all the way to Tularosa for two more."

"Sounds good to me. Where's the livery, and hotel? I need to get this horse taken care of first thing. He's about give out."

"Next street over, right behind the saloon. The hotel is up and across the street. You can't miss either one of them, but you'd better get a room as soon as you get that horse in the livery. The miners will fill this town up."

Shorty took care of the dun, and glanced at the different brands on all the horses. Two were from as far away as Montana. The Pitchfork brand from Texas was easy to spot. Then there was the Owl head from the upper Cimmiron. This one looked like an apple with two stems, and worm holes.

Shorty walked through the back door of the saloon and got himself a beer. The bar wasn't all that busy, no more than a dozen men were sitting around tables playing poker. Shorty stood against the bar and ordered himself a beer. He was standing four or five feet away from two men who had just rode in off the trail. One of them spoke in low tones, but the other's voice carried halfway across the room; he was mad as hell about something. Shorty edged a bit closer so he could hear both sides of the conversation.

The quiet one was saying, "Look, Elmore, I ain't going up against Weldon, Butch er Roy either one. You know anyone of them is better'n both of us with a gun. Darnit Elmore, we're just cowboys! And I'm not riding all the way back to Villanueva to warn Sam they're after him."

"Well, I don't like a man that'll go against his own kind. Them boys turning against Sam and his brothers just ain't right. Now you know it ain't, Bob. They've rode with 'em. For the hundredth time, you know it ain't right."

"All I'm saying Elmore, is Sam and his brothers shouldn't ought'a gone and killed that kid's family. That little sucker wears that .45 like he knows how to use it. And from the looks on that baby face of his, he ain't gonna stop 'till they're all dead. I just ain't gonna be with Sam when that happens."

Elmore was spitting mad and hollered at Bob. "Then yer not going to lift a hand to help 'em! Is that what yer saying Bob? Well, damn it, is it?"

"That's exactly what I've been trying to tell you for the past hour, Elmore. When we met up with that kid and them boys on the trail, Weldon looked me right in the eye, and told us to keep out of it. And said to keep riding south, or there'd be big trouble for us. Weldon ain't kiddin' around when he gives that look. I've know'd him too long not to believe him. I just won't go again them four fellers. No sir, I won't, never."

"Then you just sit here and do nothing! Come morning I'm riding back there and warn Sam and the boys!" Elmore stomped off to sit at a table alone.

Bob took another sip of his beer and glanced around, spotting Shorty.

"Howdy, cowboy. Buy you a beer?"

"Naw, but I appreciate the offer. I've got to get myself a room before they're all gone." Shorty stuck out his hand to shake. "I'm Shorty Thompson."

"Bob Dokes. Not from around these here parts, are you?"

"Naw, just riding through. Me and a partner have us a ranch over west of here a fair piece, just before Arizona."

"That sure sounds good. Well, I'd better get over there with Elmore, and try to talk him out of doing something pretty dang'd stupid." Bob walked over and sat down at Elmore's table. As Shorty walked out the door, he heard Elmore start in on Bob again.

By the time Shorty returned to the saloon, Pat was already sitting at a table about mid-way back. Hollering at the bartender, he waved at Shorty at the same time. Pat finished his first beer as Shorty sat down. "Get that room, Shorty?" Pat asked, as the bartender sat down two mugs of beer.

"Yeah, sure did. Say, Pat, what do you know about a couple of fellers by the names of Bob and Elmore?"

"Not much to know about them two. They're cousins. Bob wants to kind'a ride the straight trail, but Elmore is fascinated by the idea of being a badman. He spends too much time reading dime novels. They've taken up with the Kraymons and Bristols. I hate to see it, it'll either get 'em killed, or sent to prison. How did you come to know 'em?"

"I don't. I stopped in here for a beer before I got my room, and they were arguing about going to warn Sam, about Jack and them three fellers with him. Me and Bob introduced ourselves and that was about it. Bob said he wasn't going. Do you think Elmore'll ride all that way to warn Sam?"

"Yeah, could be. He's about that stupid. He probably thinks it'll get him in tight with Sam. It won't. Them Kraymon brothers are not to be trusted by no one, not even their own men. There'll be a double-cross to ever who does." Pat pushed his hat back, and tilted his chair, getting comfortable.

Shorty took a sip of beer and looked Pat in the eyes. "I'd like to ask, just why hadn't both the Kraymon and Bristol gangs been locked up? It seems like everybody knows they ain't nothing but a bunch of outlaws."

"All the witnesses are too scared, or wind up dead before a trial. I've had 'em locked up a couple of times myself, but when nobody shows up to testify against 'em, the judge had to turn 'em loose. Being a lawman, and saying this might be wrong, but it may take somebody like Jack to stop 'em."

"Well, from what Tom was telling me, if Jack and them fellers with him find the Kraymons before I do, there won't be a need for a judge." The more they talked, the more Shorty felt the need to hurry.

"Shorty, if you or Jack runs 'em back this way, I'll lock 'em up 'till you get here. I sure wish I could go with you after them, but I've got a prisoner to take to Lincoln, then go get two more down at Tularosa. Well, it's time I got some shut-eye. I've got to hit the trail pretty early, come morning." Pat pushed back his chair, and stood up.

Shorty threw the rest of his beer down his throat. "Yeah, me too. Morning is going to get here much too soon, and my ride is sure to be long and hard. Pat, you take care, and watch your back-side."

Pat wasn't in the cafe for breakfast, but Bob Dokes came in and sat with Shorty. After coffee was poured, and each of them took his first sip, Shorty asked, "Don't Elmore eat breakfast?"

"Yeah, but he cut out early. He's headed for Villanueva, over between Las Vegas and Santa Fe." Bob looked disgusted, and shook his head.

"How come you didn't ride along? I thought y'all was partners." Shorty spoke casually, and took another sip of coffee. Ham and eggs set before them.

"I went and got me a punchin' job, ridin' for Jesse Chishom's spread. Elmore should'a come too. Dumb, just plain ignorant, dumb is what he is. Gonna get hisself killed is what he'll do. Shor's rain, he's a dead man."

After breakfast Bob went east, and Shorty headed for Villanueva.

Chapter Nine

Janice, Weldon, Butch and Roy dismounted in front of the El Fidel Hotel and Emporium, in Las Vegas. Janice read the name and asked, "What in the world is an Emporium? It sounds foreign, like maybe Greek. Is it?"

Butch laughed out loud and said, "It's a fancy name for a saloon. The only difference is the price of the women and drinks. Oh, and of course the poker games have a much higher stake. That's why Weldon stopped here." Butch smiled, but saw the look on Weldon's face and quickly asked, "where to, Weldon? You name it, and we'll do it."

"I reckon we ought'a split up. You and Roy take the south side of the street, and check every saloon. Go from one end of town to the other. Me and Jack'll get us all rooms, and start working this side of the street. Hold on a minute, there's one more thing. Don't nobody rush into anything and go getting us into trouble. Work it slow and easy, one saloon, one man, one word at a time. Butch, do you and your short fuse hear me?"

"Yeah, sure, Weldon. No shooting until Jack gets there. Right?"

"All we want to do is find out where they are, and if they're here in Vegas. Jack, I want you to stick close to me. If we run into any Kraymons, they may recognize you and start shooting. Butch, Roy, we'll meet back here after dark. Good luck, and don't get too drunk, it could get you killed."

Butch smiled, "Naw, nobody knows we're working with Jack, and we'll save our drinking until later tonight. Might need a steady hand today." Roy, with a blank look on his face, was shaking his head up and down.

Butch and Roy headed across the street to Salazar's Bar and Pool hall. Weldon and Janice went into the El Fidel Hotel for their rooms. A stately looking Spanish gentleman looked up from his desk, asking, "You will be wanting a room for you and your son, no, Señor?" He was smiling.

Weldon smiled, "No, Señor. I'll be needing three rooms. One for me, and one for Jack, here, and the other for a couple of friends that'll be along later. Think you can handle that?" Weldon winked at Janice.

"Si, Señor. And will you want to stay on the Emporium floor, or the second floor, or perhaps even the third floor to get away from the noise?"

Weldon raised an eye-brow. "You got a basement, don't you?"

"Si, Señor, but you would not want to stay down there, it has no rooms. It is used only for storage, and is very damp and dark."

Weldon straightened his shoulders. "Oh, well then! We'll take the Emporium floor. That's all right with you, ain't it Jack?"

"Yeah, sure. Dang-it all Weldon! Why are you carrying on like this?"

Weldon laughed out loud. "I just wanted to see who got flustered first, you or the clerk. Your fuse is too short, Jack. Lighten up, have a little fun."

Janice smiled, "Yeah, you're right. But I knew I wasn't going to sleep in no basement with a bunch of rats, or anything else I can't see."

The clerk became very indignant. "Señor. I will have you know, we do not have rats in this establishment!" Anger flashed in his eyes.

Weldon backed off and eyed the clerk. "Hey, the kid didn't mean nothing. He was just pulling your chain to see if your bell would rang. And he done it too. Sounded good."

The old Spanish clerk smiled. "Si, Señor. He rang my bell. You are both great kidders, no?"

"Yes, Sir, we are. Say, while I'm standing here, I wonder if you'd mind answering a couple of questions for me? We're looking for a bunch of fellers, called Bristol, or maybe Kraymon. Could you tell us if they're staying here?"

The old Spaniard crossed himself. "I can tell you Señor, and thank the Blessed Mary, they are not staying here. Never will that trash stay here!"

"Y'all must not like them old boys worth a hoot. I've never heard a Spaniard call nobody trash before."

"Perhaps that was a bad choice for a word, Señor. It was said in haste.

Garbage was the word I should have used. Yes, garbage is the word."

Weldon smiled right big. "Glad you feel that'a way, feller. They ain't exactly our best friends either, huh Jack?"

"They won't be nobodies friends for much longer. Oh, Sir, could somebody bring hot water to my room? I'll be needing to take a bath."

"Señor, there is a bathroom at the end of the hallway. It also has hot and cold running water. When you are inside, just lock the door and hang out the occupied sign. No one will bother you."

Janice went to her room to get ready for her bath. Weldon dropped off his belongings and headed for the saloon for a few drinks and a little poker. The saloon was the place to start looking for the Kraymons. Not only did they gamble but they were all bad drunks.

Butch and Roy had no luck until the fifth bar they went into. There sat one of their old riding buddies. They ambled over to his table before noticing the bandage on his left leg. Butch showed a lot of concern. "Howdy, Keland. What in the world happened?"

"Oh, howdy, Butch, Roy. Sit down, have a drink. I was just about to get myself another. On that last job, I went and got myself shot. Ain't all that bad though, and Sam's taking care of me. He gave me my share just like he was suppose to, and said he'd use me again soon's I'm ready to ride. They haven't been back in for over a week, and money's running a little short, but I'll last."

Butch asked, "Then Sam and the boys ain't staying in town?"

"Naw, but I sure wish they was, I'm needing some money. They're all staying out to Villanueva. Said it was a lot closer to their work, and I guess it really is. I've heard of several stage holdups out that'a way."

"Keland, what do you say to me and Roy buying us a few rounds? We've got a good hour before we have to leave."

"That's sure a pal of you, Butch. You know, I always liked you and Roy."

"Same here, Keland. We always figgered you a friend. You wouldn't happen to know if Sam's taking on more men, would you?"

"Boy, he sure should be. In the week we've been over here, five of the boys have been killed, and four of us have got shot up pretty bad. It'll be at least two or three weeks before I'll be able to ride again."

Roy had been shaking his head up and down, or from side to side, according to what was being said at the time. He glanced at Butch, then over at Keland. "You wouldn't happen to know about how many men Sam's got riding with him right now, do you?" Roy held his head still for the answer.

"I'd say nigh on to forty or fifty. You know'd the Bristols teamed up with Sam for this big job. It'll take place this coming Saturday. That is the last of the month, ain't it?" Keland took another drink before looking at Butch and adding, "Boy, do I ever wish I could ride on this one. It'll pay more than any five or ten jobs I've ever been on. Biggest job ever. And do I ever mean the biggest! Man-o-live is it ever!" He gave out with a whistle, and laughed.

Butch sat a little straighter in his chair. "Yeah, you got that right, Saturday is the last day of the month. Sam sure must be planning something big, to let Bristol in on it."

Keland leaned closer, looking around before saying, "yeah, it's big! It's the Army payroll for Fort Marcy, over at Santa Fe! They was going to hit it halfway between Fort Union and Raton, getting both payrolls, but figgered it'd be too hard to get close enough out on them flats. It's a shame though, that Fort Union half will be good sized. Yes sir, lots of gold will be dropped off there. From what I hear, it's not only the payroll for both forts, but money to buy all their supplies for the next three months. Sam says Fort Marcy's part is well over fifty thousand dollars. How's that for a payday? Biggest ever."

Butch whistled, and Roy stopped shaking his head and sat with his eyes bugged out. Finally Roy stuttered out with, "Fifty! Did you say, fifty thousand dollars?" He shook his head from side to side. "Ain't that much money in the whole damned world, is there?" He slowly took a drink of beer.

Keland looked from one to the other, shaking his head up and down. "Yep, that's the word everybody got. Fifty thousand! Now you know why I'd like to ride on this one. I just can't with this dad-gummed shot up leg. Heck fire, it'll pay every man over five hundred dollars apiece. Are you going?"

Butch smiled, while Roy shook his head up and down. "Wouldn't miss it." Butch handed Keland a ten dollar gold piece. "This'll hold you."

Keland's eyes brightened. "Thanks, Butch, but I don't know when I'll be seeing you again. If you and Roy go on this job, when it's over, y'all will be heading for Mexico with Sam and the boys. I heard the gangs would split up, throwing the trail to the wind. Bristol's bunch will be heading for Tombstone. The whole dang U.S. Cavalry will be after them before the day is out. No witnesses left, is what I heard."

"You sit easy and take care of that leg, Keland. Me and Roy had better hook 'em. We've got a couple of things to do before riding out to Villanueva." Butch and Roy headed for the El Fidel to find Weldon and Janice.

Weldon was walking up the steps when Butch hollered at him. "Hey, Weldon, wait up! Me and Roy has some news that'll throw you for a loop."

They walked into the El Fidel Saloon and got a table out of the way so they could talk without being overheard. After ordering their drinks, Butch looked around before starting to talk. "Weldon, you ain't gonna believe who we ran into, so I'll tell you. It was Keland. He's been shot in the leg and has a lot of time on his hands and just loves to talk."

Butch stopped talking as their drinks were set on the table. After taking a quick slug of whiskey, and waiting until the waiter got out of hearing range, he smiled. "The job they're over here to pull off, is the Fort Marcy payroll. Now what do you think of that?" Butch took another drink and waited.

Weldon whistled low and long. "Boys, we could have ourselves a problem. How can we get to that many men before they try to pull this job? Sam'll be keeping everybody pretty close. Villanueva's pretty small, only one hotel with seven rooms, and two saloons. One of them's just a little hole-in-the-wall. We'll have to camp along the Pecos River, as all the rooms will be taken. No matter what we do, it's going to be touch and go.

"Dad-gum-it! I almost forgot about Janice. We'd better clue her in on what Sam's got planned. Wrong place at the right time, and we could die." Weldon rolled his eyes.

"Heck-fire, the cavalry won't be able to tell us from Sam and his boys. Did you say this takes place Saturday? Fellers, we've got a lot to do."

"Yeah, that's what Keland told us. What do you have in mind?" Butch was getting worried about all the men that were going to die. Some would be his friends, but still, he was glad he and Roy were riding with Janice. Roy seemed to feel the tension, he hadn't shaken his head in ten minutes.

Weldon looked around and asked, "Did either of you see Janice?" Neither one had, so Weldon wrinkled his brow. "I wonder what kind of trouble that little dickens has gone and gotten herself into? Let's hit the street and look until we find her. Hell, she's trouble."

As they threw their drinks down their throats and pushed back their chairs, in walked, Janice wearing a new Stetson, boots, and new clothes.

Weldon looked at her with a frown on his face. She stopped smiling at once and asked, "What's the matter? Don't my clothes fit? My hat's all right, ain't it? Well, somebody say something! You don't like it! That's it, I can tell it, you don't like it!"

Butch and Roy sat back down, as Weldon caught Janice by her left arm and walked her over to a mirror. "Now that don't look like Jack to me. Does it to you?" Weldon put his hands on his hips, watching her eyes in the mirror.

It took Janice a full minute to figure out what Weldon was talking about. Even though the shirt was too large, through the thin white material, her small nipples were very plainly visible. She turned red and slapped her hand to her mouth, elbows covering her small breasts. "Oh my God! What am I going to do? I can't walk back outside this way! Oh my God. Darn, darn it to heck!"

Weldon smiled, "Don't panic, just walk down the hallway to your room and change shirts. No one has noticed you yet, or they'd followed you to see where you were going." Weldon stood with his hands on his hips as Janice rushed down the hallway and into her room, slamming the door.

Going back and sitting with Roy and Butch, Weldon spoke in a low even tone. "Fellers, this won't ever be brought up again. Get my drift?"

"Sure Weldon, we wouldn't'a said anything noway. We're just sorry she didn't save herself that embarrassment by not catching that before she left the store. She's a darn'd good kid." Roy's head was shaking up and down.

Five minutes later Janice walked in and sat across from Weldon. She was a little red faced, but didn't say a word. Weldon went right on talking like nothing had happened. "Jack, we've got us a few problems. It seems as though the Kraymons have teamed up with the Bristols to rob the army payroll. If we're seen with or near any of them, the cavalry is going to think we're some of the gang. We've got to stop and think all of this through. They're out at Villanueva until after the robbery, then they'll split up and head for Mexico. If we ride for Villanueva now, we'll have to camp out down by the Pecos River.

"All of the rooms in town will already be full. Also, we can't all go into town together. They'll be needing men, but wonder why we're wanting to join upon something this big and dangerous. We're open to anything you might have to say. We've got to come up with something so we won't all get killed. Sam's got about forty men. Maybe more."

Janice looked apprehensive. "Weldon, I'm not going to stop now. The cavalry is not going to cheat me out of killing everyone of them Kraymons, and whoever else that gets in my way while I'm doing it. How long do we have before they pull this robbery, and where will it happen?"

"Three days from now, they're going to hit the payroll coach over by Tecolote. That's about three hours southwest of here by coach. And another thing, we're not going to stop trying to stop them. It's just that we have to take it kind'a easy. I don't want any of us winding up getting killed, much less all of us. We'll think of something tonight and tomorrow, then ride out that way and look at the set-up. Does that sound all right to you, Jack? It's your call."

"Yeah, that sounds fine to me. But right now I'm starving to death. Let's get out of here and find something to eat. Where do y'all want to go?"

"Right here. They got darn good food. I'll catch a waiter's attention."

They ate supper and talked about the coming robbery. Except Janice hadn't said a word. Weldon realized something was wrong and asked, "something on your mind that we ought'a know about, Jack?"

"Naw, I guess not. It's just that all of this riding has about caught up with me, and I'm bone tired. If y'all don't mind, I think after supper I'll head for a good night's sleep. Are y'all staying up for awhile?" Janice looked from face to face as she stood to leave. She yawned and put her hand over her mouth.

Weldon smiled and said, "Yeah, there's a big poker game somewhere in here with my name on it. Butch and Roy are going to sit in for a few hands just to get it started. But don't worry about us, we don't need as much sleep as you youngsters do. We'll see you in the morning for breakfast."

Janice went to her room and sat on the edge of the bed. "Lord, what am I going to do? What if the cavalry kills all the Kraymons before I get my chance? It's gotta be me Lord, it's gotta be me!" Slowly she went over all her options in her mind. She could wait until after the robbery and then take up the trail of ever who might be left alive? No, she might lose them between here and Mexico. Should she warn the cavalry so they would have enough men along to wipe out the whole gang? No, if she did that, she wouldn't get the Kraymons. Lying back on the bed, she closed her eyes.

Mumbling to herself before dropping off to sleep. "I've got to do it."

The next morning at breakfast Janice acted like she had ants in her pants. Weldon and Butch were carrying on a conversation that had nothing to do with the Kraymons. Roy was sitting all bug-eyed, taking in every word. He would look from one to the other, then shake his head up and down, or from side to side. It didn't take long for Janice to get enough of that talk. Standing, she slapped her hand down hard on the table, all wide-eyed and mad. All three men jumped, and had their hands on their gun butts.

"All right, dad-gum-it! Y'all have figured out a way to leave me behind! I can tell it! Wellll, it ain't going to happen that way, so you may as well 'fess up and tell me all about it!" With her hands on her hips, she blurted out, "Weldon, are you going to tell me, or do I have to stick to you like a boil on your bottom? And don't think I won't!"

"Just hold your horses, Jack. Nobody's made up their minds to do anything. Another hour waiting for you, then we might have had to."

"I'm sorry. It's just that I thought... well, never mind what I thought. But we do have to come up with something darned fast, today is Thursday."

Weldon cleared his throat. Butch moved his chair back several inches, and Roy stopped shaking his head. "Jack, I know you're going to have a wall-eyed, barn-kicking fit, but it would be best if a couple of us rode out there and looked things over. If everything looks all right, one of us will come and get you. I mean it, Jack. It'd be for the best." Weldon never took his eyes off her.

Janice looked him in the eyes. "If that's what you think is best, well so be it. I'll wait here until you come for me. When will you be leaving?"

All three men sat with their mouths open. Weldon cleared his throat before saying, "Well, we figured me and Butch should ride out there tomorrow morning. Roy will stay in town with you. That's just in case some of them boys show up back here, and you want to day-light 'em. Say, wait a minute. How come you're not laying on the floor kicking and screaming, throwing a full fledged fit?"

"Oh, I don't know. I just figured I'd better come to my senses and listen to y'all for a change. It might save my life. Being as we're not going to do anything today, I think I'll ride out towards Watrous. I heard a big rancher has built two of the biggest hay barns in the world. They're supposed to be over thirty feet tall, and maybe a hundred feet long. I don't remember, but I think I was told they were forty feet wide, also. Anyway, that will keep me busy most of the day, and I don't have to sit and watch y'all play poker."

"If we're not here, we'll be down at the Castanada Hotel and Saloon." Weldon warned Janice, "Now Jack, you ride with both eyes open going out that'a way. There's some mighty nasty fellers what rides the Santa Fe Trail."

"I'll be careful, but I'm riding wide of the trail. I'll be cutting across country." Janice smiled right big, and then said, "It'll be awhile before I ride out. I've got to go by the barber shop and get a hair cut. Mine's a little long."

Butch laughed, "Yeah, for a boy, but not for a pretty girl. But you go ahead, it'll be best so nobody'll start thinking just how pretty you really are."

Janice paid for their meal before walking out the door. On the sidewalk she looked east then west, seeing the barber shop six doors up. She was the first customer of the day. The barber was a chubby, jolly man and completely bald headed. As Janice sat in the chair, he remarked, "I see you didn't come in for a shave, young man?" He smiled right big.

"No Sir, but I do need a hair cut. It looks like you cut your own hair a might short. I just want mine off my neck and ears."

The barber slapped his leg and roared in laugher. "That's a good one! By Jacks I'll have to remember that one. Thought I'd heard 'em all, but that's one a new one on me."

After her hair cut, Janice looked into the mirror. Except for her full lips, she saw her twin brother Jack. She was proud and thanked the barber. Going back to the El

Fidel, she slipped in the back door, and went to her room. As she threw her things together, she wondered what Weldon would do when they found her gone. Opening the door, she stuck her head out and looked down the hallway. No one was around as she stepped out the back door and ran down the alley. At the next street, she cut back south and headed for the livery. Twice she looked over her shoulder, but saw no one she knew.

Her head kept turning as she saddled her horse. The hostler noticed her nervous actions and asked, "You running from somebody, boy?"

Janice hadn't seen him walk up on her left side and almost jumped out of her boots. "Huh? Oh no! I'm not running from nobody. It's just that I've got to get home, or Papa's gonna be all fired mad."

The old man chuckled out loud. "Yeah, I know what you mean. You stayed in town a little too long, didn't you? Well, when I's a kid like you, I use to do the same thing, and more than once. Got my britches tanned plenty of times for it too. I'd bet you got yourself a little girlfriend around here abouts, huh? Them pretty girls can get a boy in too much trouble with his pa, can't they boy? Wouldn't you say so?"

The old man waited for Janice to answer him. "That about right, boy?"

"No, Sir. My Pa never whipped me, and I don't have no girlfriend. But he's sure grabbed me by my arm and told me not to do whatever, again. Well, I'd best be riding. I'll see you when I get back to town. So long."

"What happened to those men you rode in with?"

"They're about, probably playing poker. They work for Pa."

Janice swung into her saddle and hit a fast, long lope. She was headed for Villanueva. It would be late tonight before Weldon, Butch and Roy figured out she was gone. Then it would be too late, she would be in Villanueva with a gang of outlaws before noon today. Maybe have a Kraymon or two, dead.

At almost the same time Janice rode through Romeroville, Elmore left Anton Chico. He would beat her to Villanueva by just under two hours. Shorty, with a tired butt, was two hours behind Elmore, riding easy, but still in a hurry. He needed to find Jack and his friends.

Janice rode into Villanueva and tied up in front of a large saloon. Dismounting, she stepped on the board walkway, then changed her mind and took her horse to the livery. A young boy was combing a horse's tail, and looked up. "Can I do something for you?"

Janice stepped down, as she was saying, "Yeah, I need this horse stalled for a few days." She looked about, and didn't like anything she had seen of Villanueva. It appeared to be a hard, tough little village. What the heck, she wasn't staying very long.

"We don't got no stalls left. But I can put him out in the lot."

"Naw, that's all right. I'll just tie her up here at the hitch-rail. You feed her here and take her to water after awhile. When will you have a stall?"

"Soon's Mister Garcia comes for his horse. Maybe an hour at the most."

"That'll be fine. Stall her then. Now you'll do that, won't you?" Janice watched the young boy's face as he tightened his lips.

"Yeah, sure thing, I'll... stall... him... then." He was looking past Janice.

Janice turned, and walking toward her was Elmore and two other men. They were no more than fifty feet away when Elmore stopped and went for his gun. He never cleared his holster before he was slammed back, dead. Janice stood with her smoking pistol still in her hand and pointed toward the other two. Both of them kept their hands away and clear of their weapons. The youngest of the two shouted, "What was that all about? You going and killing Elmore that'a way!" His hand hovered above, but away from his gun-butt. He wanted to draw so bad, his hand hurt, but his brain just wouldn't let him do it.

With a slow even voice, Janice answered, "I was under the impression Elmore was about to gun me down. Now in all good conscience, I just couldn't let him do that. Do either of you two want to take up where he left off? If not, I'll put my gun away." She looked both of them in the eyes.

Both men very slowly put the thong over the hammer of their guns, then moved their hands away. The older of the two spoke up. "Naw, Kid. We didn't owe Elmore nothing. He couldn't finish his own fight, we shor's heck ain't going to try and do it for him. Without getting you riled, where'd you learn to use a .45 like that? That's about the best I've ever seen."

Janice smiled a wicked little smile. "I started learning the day I busted out of Leavenworth Prison."

The older of the two, glanced at his young partner, then back at Janice, saying, "Leavenworth! That's a Military Prison, kid!"

Janice narrowed her eyes. "I know what kind of prison it is, and I ain't no kid! I'm nineteen years old. Three years ago I got sent up for whittling on a Captain. The old boy slapped me, and out weighed me by a hundred and fifty pounds. I whipped out my Bowie and worked him over just a might. While I was behind bars, some men with the know-how, told me to start using a gun. It's a lot cleaner, and now I use a gun about as well as anyone around, don't you agree? " Janice had that crooked little smile on her face again.

Both men shook their heads up and down. "Yeah, that's for dang sure." The older man stuck out his hand to shake. "I'm Hap, and this is Doug. What'er you called, feller?"

"Uh, uh, Ben! Ben Keechum! Yeah, that's it, Ben Keechum."

"Well Ben, come on over to the saloon, I'd like to buy you a drink. Gets kind'a boring around this one horse place. Not even enough whores to go around. Sam won't be back for another... Here he comes now. I'll introduce y'all. Maybe he could use another fast gun. I figgered that's why Elmore showed back up here wanting to talk with Sam. He just never got the chance. He never was too smart, far as I could tell."

Sam Kraymon and three men dismounted. Grimacing, Janice wanted to blast everyone of them right where they stood. Sam walked over and looked down at Elmore. Looking at Hap, he asked, "Who drilled Elmore?"

"This here kid went and done it. I mean Ben, Ben's his name. And he went and done it after Elmore started his draw. Sam, I want you to meet Ben Keechum, the fastest, littlest gun I ever saw. I mean it Sam, the fastest!"

Sam stuck out his hand. "Howdy, Ben. Think I might have I seen you around before. Have I?"

"No, Sir. I'm not from around these parts at all."

"Hummm, must have been somebody that looks like you. Your face has a familiar roundness to it. Oh well, let's get out of this sun and get a drink."

Janice walked easily as they went through the saloon door. Everyone ordered his drink, and Janice got a sarsaparilla. One of the younger men started to snicker, but one sharp look from Janice cut it short. Sam and Hap stopped by the bar and talked, while Doug and Janice went to a table. They both noticed how their man backed down at Ben's stare. "Sam snorted, "Hap, I'm telling you, that little shit had better be as fast as you said he was."

Sam pulled up a chair and sat down. Taking a quick slug of whiskey, he asked, "What'er you doing out this'a way, Ben?"

"Oh, just riding through, and staying off the main trails. Never know who you might run in to out this way. I'm kind'a a loner."

"You wouldn't happen to be interested in a quick job, come Saturday, would you? If you're as good with that gun as Hap says you are, you could make a fast five hundred. Think you could handle that?"

Janice gave a surprised look that made Sam think asking was a mistake.

"Five hundred dollars! Heck yeah, I'm interested. Which army do I have to kill for that much money?" Janice made her eyes big, and looked greedy.

Sam chuckled at the spunk of the young boy. "Oh, I don't know, about half of the U.S. Cavalry, that's all. I'll tell you what, Ben, if Saturday comes off as well as I've got planned, we're going to take over fifty thousand dollars of cavalry money. It'll be worth five hundred to every man that rides with us. After the robbery, we all meet at Lamy for the split. Some of us will be headed for Mexico, down the Rio Grande. The others will go into Mexico by way of Tombstone. By splitting up, the cavalry won't know where to look. You can ride with whoever you want." Sam sat back and watched Janice's face.

She had butterflies in her stomach, but was firm with her answer. "I'll ride with you, where I can stick close to all that money. I wouldn't want my five hundred going to Mexico without me." They all laughed, and Sam slapped her on the shoulder. Janice eyed them all as she sipped her sarsaparilla, wanting to gun all of them right now.

"You're all right, kid. You'll make it in this world, and looking out for number one is the only way to do it." Sam sat back and smiled.

Shorty rode into Villanueva as Elmore's body was being loaded into a wagon. Sitting on his dun in front of the livery, he turned his head back to the wagon. "I wonder if Elmore got to tell Sam Kraymon what he wanted to?"

The hostler walked up and said, "Mister, if you're looking for a stable for your horse, there ain't one. I'm all full up. I can feed and water him's all."

"Yeah, I needed one, but it can wait. What happened to Elmore?"

"Elmore wasn't as fast as he thought he was. He tried to draw against the littlest gun I ever saw, and lost. That kid's faster'n greased lightning. Elmore had already started his draw, and never got to finish it."

"What was this kid's name?"

"Told Sam it was Ben Keechum. Ever hear of him?"

"Naw, can't say as I have. When might you have an empty stall? I sure hate to leave this dun out, unless I have to. Any other place around here with a barn?" Shorty didn't like leaving the dun out in the open.

"Nobody else has a barn, and I won't have a empty stall until Saturday. Then they'll all be empty. Both the Kraymon and Bristol bunches are going off to rob the army payroll."

"Rob the payroll! How did you hear something like that?" Shorty dismounted, watching the hostler look all around before answering.

"Heck fire, I thought everybody know'd about that. They been here for over a week, robbing and killing travelers over on the Santa Fe Trail. They just been hanging around, waiting for the big one. And man, from what I hear, this is the big one. When outlaws get drunk, they like to brag, and talk their heads off. Some more than others."

Shorty tied his dun at the hitch-rail, beside a beautiful sorrel mare.

Walking over, he looked at the brand, then asked the hostler, "Who's riding the Whip Cord Brand? I ain't never seen it in these parts before."

The hostler let go with a half cup of tobacco juice at a fence post before saying, "That horse belongs to the kid what killed Elmore. Fast little sucker. Littlest gun totter I've ever seen. Uh huh, deadly fast."

"You wouldn't happen to know where I could find him, would you?"

"Yep. When Sam Kraymon rode in and saw Elmore laying face down, he asked who done it. Hap and Doug, they're two of Sam's men, told how fast the kid was with his .45. Sam took him to the saloon to buy him a drink. Knowing Sam as I do, the kid will be riding with him come Saturday morning."

Shorty thanked the hostler and walked to the saloon. The whole place was full of hard cases. Shorty ordered a beer and stood with his back to the bar. He slowly eyed the room without being conspicuous. At a table about halfway back, he spotted the youngest person in the room, and almost busted out laughing. Anyone who had ever seem Alice McCord, would have to know this good-looking kid had to be hers. Alice was a beautiful woman, and Henry McCord had been a lucky man to find her.

Shorty finished his beer, and got another before walking back to Kraymon's table. Four men were playing poker, while Janice watched, looking so bored she was nodding. Holding his beer in his left hand, Shorty asked, "I noticed you were one man short for a good game. Would any of you mind if I sit in?" He took a sip of beer and waited.

Sam looked up at the young man. "You're right, we are one man short. Sit down, sit down. Ben, move over and let the man have a chair. I'm Sam. This is Ben, Doug, Hap, and my brother Nick. The game's five card draw. Dollar limit 'til the last card's draw'd, then it's how ever much you want to lose." Everyone but Janice, chuckled at Sam's wit.

Shorty sat down and glanced around the table at everyone. Janice swallowed hard and moved a few inches farther away from Shorty. When Jim Woodard rode up in her yard, she had thought he was pretty, but this young man sitting next to her was plumb handsome. Her face had flushed a bit as she asked, "What's your name, feller?"

"Oh, I'm sorry. I was so interested in getting into the game, I forgot to say. It's Ben, Ben Cord."

Sam was dealing the cards, and stopped his hands dead still. "Well now, if that don't beat all. Two total strangers come riding in, and both of them is named Ben."

He looked at Shorty, closely. "Said your name was Cord, right?" Not waiting for Shorty to answer, he turned to Janice. "And you said your name was Keechum, right? And neither of you are from New Mexico?"

Shorty answered, "Naw, I'm from Texas, headed for Tombstone. Heard they was hiring guns down that way." He looked each man in the eye.

Janice knew he could hear her heart beating. When a young man started doing this to her, she knew she was becoming a woman. God, she couldn't take her eyes off him. She had to get out of here, now! She couldn't trust herself to talk anymore. She was afraid she would start cooing if he said another word to her. She closed her eyes, and swallowed hard, hoping he would disappear, or just get up and leave.

Janice scooted back her chair and said, "I think I'm going to get some shut-eye. I've been on the trail too long, and am dead tired."

Sam glanced up from his cards saying, "All the rooms are taken. If you'd like, you can bunk with me and my brother Nick."

"Naw, thanks. I'll throw my roll on the bank of the Pecos. I noticed a nice little tree-lined cove, and I like sleeping outside in the fresh air. All of this smoke is tearing my head off. I'll see y'all for breakfast."

Everyone told her, yeah, and Shorty said, "I might just come out and bunk by you, if that's all right. This smoke tightens my throat, also."

Janice tried hard not to blush. "Yeah, sure, if you want to. It's a couple hundred yards down stream from here. There's a lot of trees where it'll block the wind." She got up and walked out the door.

She got to her horse just as the hostler was about to put him in a stall. "I thought you wanted him stalled? I've lost customers already." The hostler was a bit put out. "I ought'a charge you something anyway!"

"Yeah, I did, but all the rooms are taken, so I have to camp down by the River." Janice took the reins and led her horse slowly away, then stopped and pitched back a dollar. What was she going to do? What was she going to talk to Ben about? "I wish he wouldn't come. That's funny, his name is Cord, and mine is McCord. God, I sure wish he wasn't an outlaw. I think I'd like to get to know him better, I mean when I'm through killing the Kraymons. Oh Lord, what if he joins up with them?"

Janice walked to the cove and set up camp. After finding driftwood, she built a fire and started her supper. She was thinking about how nice looking and clean cut Ben was, when she heard twigs snapping under someone's foot. It was still light enough to see a large, tall man walking toward her camp. She could tell he was drunk by the way he was swaggering. Before she could think of anything to say, the man spoke up.

"Sam said you was coming down here to camp. Said you didn't want to bunk with us, but I want you to. You see, I like little boys. I have me a woman ever now and again, but they ain't nothing like a boy. Know what I mean?"

Janice kept her hand close to her .45, and said, "I thought you was one of them that raped that McCord woman and killed her. Least ways that's what I was told. Sam said you was his brother, Nick. He was right, wasn't he?"

"Yeah, that's me, and I done it. I'd bet you're better'n she'd ever be."

Janice set her jaw, hard. "Well, why don't we just find out! You get out of your clothes while I get my bedroll all laid out." Her heart was beating like a thousand drums. This was another Kraymon she was going to kill now, and be done with him. Another low life stinking swamp rat, dead. "Don't take so much time, I'm ready to do it, now!"

"Now you're talking, kid. I told Sam you'd go along with what I wanted to do, I could tell. I'll be easy, and if you like it, we'll do it again later on."

Janice got a little cocky. "Oh, I know I'll like it, and I'll do it again!"

Nick took his gun-belt off, hanging it over a low limb. Sitting on a rock, he removed his boots, then stood and took off his pants and shirt. Turning his back to Janice, he walked ten feet to the river and proceeded to take a leak. Janice watched his every move, and was ready when he turned around. She had her shirt unbuttoned, and the shirt- tail pulled back. Nick tried to focus his eyes on two, small, perfect breasts. "Dang, where'd you get them, kid?"

Janice spoke through clinched teeth. "I growed 'em, you idiot! And before you die, I wanted you to know something! I'm Janice McCord, the daughter of Alice McCord! You, Nick Kraymon, are nothing but a no good raping, murdering skunk!"

Nick opened his mouth and was starting to talk, when Janice drew her gun and shot him three times in the groin. Grabbing his crotch and dropping to his knees, she shot him in the mouth, knocking him backward into the swift running river. Walking over, she looked into the water, but the body never surfaced. Hurrying as fast as she could, she threw his gun-belt and clothes in after him. Looking around to make sure no one could tell he had been there, she sat down beside her fire and went on with supper.

Five minutes later a couple of men walked up and looked the camp over. "Say, kid, did you hear any shooting down this way? Sounded like four or five shots was fired."

Janice stood with her right hand inches away from her gun. "Naw, it sounded like it came from out on the trail somewhere. All I heard was a faint echo." She was calmly eating a biscuit, left handed, showing little interest.

As they walked off down river, Janice was humming a tune her father use to hum. "That was a lovely song. I wonder how it went?" She finished eating her supper, and lay on her bedroll. Even the stars looked a bit bigger and brighter tonight. Yes, a lovely night.

Chapter Ten

Shorty rode into Janice's camp, and unsaddled his dun. Dropping his bedroll across the fire from where Janice lay, he asked, "How long have you been riding with this bunch of cut-throats, Ben? Couldn't be too long, you're a little bit young to have a name yet. A fast gun and hard name is what it takes."

Janice was sitting cross-legged, staring into the fire. "Just today. After I killed Elmore, and they saw how fast I am with my gun, Sam thought he could use me on this job." She looked at Shorty's face and asked, "You hire on?"

"Naw, I thought about it, but figured President Hayes would get plenty mad if one of his Marshals started robbing U.S. Army payrolls. You know, It'd look bad and set a bad example. One Marshal starts it, then they'd all expect to be able to do the same thing. And all that robbing would sooner or later interfere with enforcing the law. Wouldn't you think?" Shorty watched her as he rubbed down his dun.

"Huh? Yeah, oh yeah! But you said 'his Marshals'. Is that what you're trying to tell me, you're a U.S. Marshal? You don't look old enough to be no Marshal. You're not much older than I am. Wait a minute! I know you, don't I! Well son-of-a-gun!"

Shorty laughed and reached over the fire to shake hands. "Yeah, Jack, I'm your cousin, Shorty Thompson."

"Shorty! How did you find me? How did you know it was me? Did you come to help, or take me back to Lincoln? Oh God, am I ever glad to see you! Well, are you going to talk, or just stand there?"

"Now that you gave me a chance, I'll talk. First off, me and Norval got you cleared of killing your folks. As far as finding you, you were supposed to be riding with Weldon Rose and a couple more fellers. I came over because I heard the Kraymons and Bristols had teamed up to rob an army payroll. And yes, I'm going to help you, but where's Weldon, Butch and Roy? Are they here? I didn't see them in town."

"They're in Las Vegas. They'll be high-tailing it in here come morning. And about mad enough to spit bullets. Right about now they're finding out I'm gone. I'd bet Weldon is having a calf right this instant. You'd think he was my mother, the way he hovers over me. I had to come out here and join up with Sam, so I could get close enough to kill the rest of the Kraymons. I killed Nick about thirty minutes ago." Janice smiled her crooked little smile, and watched for Shorty to choke.

"You what?" Shorty was dumbfounded, and couldn't believe his ears.

"Yeah, I killed him right here, not thirty minutes ago. He came walking into camp, saying he liked little boys. He thought I should sleep with him tonight, and he didn't care all that much for women. When he got undressed, I told him who I was, and shot him. Three more Kraymons is all I got to go. Boy, is this ever fun, just like killing rats."

Shorty was watching Janice's face every second. It was as hard as stone. "Jack, you've got to be careful. When they find out that Nick is missing, there'll be a lot of trouble. Me and you are the only new comers. We'll be looked at almighty hard. You'd better know what you've gone and done."

"Shorty, I don't care what they do. If they think they can take me in a gunfight, I know six men that try will be dead with me. If Weldon don't mess up my plan, when Saturday gets here, and the shooting starts, I'll be back shooting every Kraymon I can get in my sights. Every stinking one of them!"

Shorty looked at Janice's set jaw. He didn't know how he could talk the boy into letting him jail every man he could. Jack had to realize the Kraymons must be taken alive and stand trial before the judge in Lincoln. "Jack, you know you can't just go shooting men in the back. It's just not done that way. We need to take them to trial and send them to the hangman. And only after they are found guilty."

"Shorty, you didn't see what those men did to my mother! Much less my bro..., sister and dad! I'll kill them anyway I can; when they're asleep, riding away from me, or eating a meal across the table. I want to make this very clear to you, I'm going to kill everyone of the Kraymons, or anyone else that gets in my way while I'm doing it! If it takes robbing an army payroll to get it done, so be it. You see, no matter what it takes, I'll do." Tears glistened.

"Whoa, now hold on Jack. I can understand you being bitter, but with your frame of mind, you'll wind up getting yourself killed. Don't think for one minute that the cavalry is going to stand by and be robbed. They're going to be shooting back with everything they've got, and some of those old boys have fought Indians and outlaws for years. They're trained to get that army payroll though." Shorty watched her face for a reaction, and saw only cold, hard, total determination.

"Then what do you have in mind? When Weldon and them get here, y'all can figure out how to stop the robbery, and I'll figure out how to get the Kraymons. "She looked at him, and said, "I think y'all will have it worse."

"Let's get some shut-eye. Maybe we can come up with something by morning." Shorty was bone tired, and worried about Jack's outlook. He was determined enough to get himself into serious trouble, or even killed.

Shorty had coffee on before it was light in the east. He looked over at Jack, and thought of how this boy's life had changed since his parents and sister were killed. He looked like a little kid laying there asleep. No kid his age should have to go through what he was. His heart must be broken.

Janice smelled the coffee, and woke up. Leaning on one elbow and rubbing her eyes, she asked, "Did you come up with anything yet? We have got to do something in a hurry. Times running out."

"Yeah, I'm riding to Fort Union and warn the cavalry so they'll have enough men to handle whatever. How many men does Kraymon have?"

Shorty glanced across the fire at Janice. "How come you slept in all your clothes, Jack? Gets awful hot, don't it?"

"Yeah, but I didn't know if I'd have to leave in a hurry." Janice needed to go somewhere in a hurry, and relieve herself, bad. "Are you going to fix breakfast here, or do we go to the cafe? I'm about half starved this morning."

Shorty laughed, "I've got plenty for both of us. I'll just fix breakfast here. I'd bet that cafe will be full for hours, feeding that many men."

Janice chuckled out loud. "Yeah, I bet that's so, and I'd rather eat out here, it'll probably be better food. Oh yeah, between the Bristols and Kraymons, there's at least forty-six men." Janice thought of how she could get away and go down stream for a few minutes. "Shorty, while you're cooking breakfast, I think I should walk down river aways and make sure Nick's body didn't hang up on a snag. You know, make sure it's gone."

Shorty was unloading his pack and said, "Yeah, that is not a bad idea. I'll bet they search the riverbanks first thing. They might just think he was so drunk he fell in. That is unless they find his body shot full of bullet holes."

Janice walked down stream for several hundred yards, then cut into a closely grown salt cedar thicket. She had just finished pulling up her pants when she heard two men arguing and walking straight toward her position. Dropping to her knees, she scooted out of sight of the riverbank.

As they passed her position, one of them was saying, "Dang-it Jess, I don't care what he said his name was! I've seen that dun stud over in Kelley, and a U.S. Marshal was riding him. It's gotta be the same horse. Let's just walk right up to him and ask what he's doing over this way. Won't hurt, and him and that kid are camped up here by the river."

As the men walked up stream toward Shorty, Janice circled around to the north. She would come in behind camp and be in the trees, unseen. She wouldn't be able to get there first and warn Shorty, but she could lend a hand if any shooting started. She bent low and ran as fast as she could.

Shorty saw the men approaching, and remembered seeing them in the saloon last night. "Howdy, Jess, Culp. Care for a cup of coffee? I just made it fresh." Shorty's .45 was on his hip and ready for use.

"Howdy, Ben. Where's Ben? By looking at them horses, I see y'all camped together. Y'all hadn't seen Nick, have you?" Both men felt easier that the other Ben wasn't in camp. They had heard how fast he was with his side-arm. Jess was looking around as he spoke. "Yeah, if you got a extra cup, I'll have some. What about you Culp?"

"Yeah, one cup'll be fine." Culp then made the mistake of lifting his gun an inch in it's holster. Shorty was ready for trouble, as he poured their coffee. He knew outlaws, none were to be trusted.

Janice came walking from the trees, and was making enough noise to shatter any thoughts that Jess and Culp had of gunning Shorty. "Howdy Culp, Jess. Hope y'all saved me a little of that coffee. I ain't had none yet, nor any breakfast. Are y'all staying for breakfast? I'm sure between us, we have plenty of food. Ben told me he was a good cook, and that cafe should be so full you can't get in." Janice kept talking as she accepted a cup of coffee from Shorty. "So, Jess, your brother Sam sure must have the brains to work up a job as big as this one. I'll sure be glad when it's over. I can use my five hundred, how about you? Being Sam's brother, I'd bet you get a lot bigger cut than the rest of us, huh? Yeah, I bet so, huh?"

Jess's face went hard, as he shifted his coffee to his left hand. "Being kind'a nosy, ain't you kid? Questions like that ain't asked of a man. 'Specially from a kid that just rode in yesterday. Now, have y'all seen Nick?"

Janice stiffened. "Don't get testy, Jess! Y'all are the first to visit our camp this morning. We ain't seen nobody else. I didn't mean to seem nosy, I'm just excited about tomorrow. I ain't never seen five hundred at one time."

Shorty was standing with his mouth open. He couldn't figure out why Jack was carrying on this way. Jess and Culp knew this wasn't the time to confront Shorty, so

Jess poured the last of his coffee on the ground. "Culp, we'd better get on up to the cafe and eat before it's all gone. Well, you two Bens take it easy, and we'll see y'all in the saloon later." They walked off.

When they were out of hearing range, Shorty asked, "What was that all about Jack? I thought I was going to have to shoot you to get you to shut up."

"I overheard them talking when they passed me, and that's what they wanted to do to you, shoot you. Culp remembered seeing your dun over at Kelley, and told Jess a U.S. Marshal was riding him. I was afraid they'd catch you bent over cooking breakfast, and back shoot you. Yeah, and that's all I need, you getting shot."

"Naw, I heard them coming, but thinks for coming out of those trees when you did. I thought I'd seen Culp before, I just couldn't think of where."

Janice sat on her heels, drinking coffee. "What are you going to do now? They have strong suspicions about you." Even if Shorty was her cousin, she sure thought he was handsome, and felt all fluttery and feminine inside.

"It's not as much what I'm going to do, as what you're going to do. I'm riding for Fort Union, and am asking you to ride with me. And there's no telling when Weldon and them will get here." Shorty though to himself, "This boy's my cousin, but man, he looks like a sissy. Darned near plumb pretty."

"I'm not going with you, but if you're not back by the time we ride out, I'll not ride against the cavalry. My horse will come up lame, or I'll think of something else. I'll hold back and pick myself out a good vantage spot where

I can't miss the Kraymons when the shooting starts. My biggest worry is Weldon, he'll be having a conniption fit. Look! Here comes Weldon and Butch, now. They must have left Las Vegas three or four hours ago. Man, am I in for it! Don't leave until I can cool him down just a bit. He'll want to tan my hide, but good." Janice seemed to pale just a little.

Weldon and Butch brought their horses to a sliding halt fifteen feet away. Weldon sat in his saddle, with his eyes glaring at Janice, then at Shorty. "Jack, for Christ sakes! What are you trying to do, get your fool self killed? And who's this feller you've taken up with? Do you know anything about him? You can't just side with strangers this way. And to beat that, I told you to never trust nobody!" Weldon was visibly mad, but you could also tell he was sincerely worried about Janice.

"This is my cousin, U.S. Marshal, Shorty Thompson."

Weldon and Butch dismounted, and Weldon was still mad. "If you ever pull another stunt like the one you just did, I don't care who's with you, I'll tan your hide until your nose bleeds buttermilk! Do I make myself clear?"

"Yes, Weldon, I hear you. And I'm sorry about deceiving you, but I had to get in with the Kraymons. Oh, I had to kill Elmore yesterday. He recognized me from out on the trail. He tried to draw down on me, but wasn't fast enough. Evidently I got him before he could tell anyone about me. I'm in pretty solid with Sam, because of my fast gun. Oh yeah, and before I forget, I killed Nick Kraymon last night." There came her crooked little smile.

"You did what?" Shorty poured Weldon and Butch some coffee. Weldon took a swallow and said, "Shorty, now you see what we're up against. She's, I mean, he's going to kill all the Kraymons and Bristols. We're trying to figure out a way to help. Butch here has rode with them until lately. Him and Roy can get right in, but what about Janice? She can't... I mean, Jack here can't seem to understand just how dangerous these fellers are."

If Shorty heard the slip of tongue, he paid no attention. "It looks like a man called Culp, recognized my dun stud. I don't think I should go back into town. I'm heading for Fort Union to warn the cavalry. If anyone ask where I'm at, just tell them I rode off. I'm going to have to push pretty hard to make it. I'll probably be riding with the cavalry, so don't none of y'all take a shot at me. Remember I'm riding the big dun, so when the shooting starts, try to miss me. Now, let's eat. I'm starved."

After breakfast Shorty saddled up and headed for Fort Union as fast as he could push his dun. It was less than fifty miles, but he wanted to reach Las Vegas and see if the payroll coach was staying all night there. If it wasn't in Las Vegas, he would ride east and meet it on the plains. If there wasn't enough guards, he would ride on to the fort and talk with General Russell. Shorty mumbled, "I still think General Russell is a weird bird. He don't look like he could teach school, much less command a army post."

The moment Shorty rode out of sight, Weldon started in on Janice. "Janice, sit down, and don't say a word until I'm finished with you! Whether you remember it or not, we're all in this to the end. What you have to keep in mind, we have to work together, or none of us will come out alive. What you did was just plain selfish and stupid. These men we're up against care no more for human life than if they were swatting a mosquito. From here on out, you're sticking close to me and Butch. Roy waited in Las Vegas to see if you showed up there. He'll be along in a couple of hours, and will have a word or two to say also. Dad-gum-it, you had us worried to death! We didn't know but what you went off and got yourself shot. All right, that's all I have to say. You can talk if you want to, but be mighty careful, I'm still mad."

"You had better believe I want to talk!" Janice had her hands on her hips. Smiling, she quietly said, "Thanks fellows, for worrying. I'm sorry, and it won't happen again. But you see, I had to do something. The thought of the cavalry getting the Kraymons first...!"

Butch had patiently waited until Weldon was through talking to Janice. "Now it's my turn! Janice, I was so dad-gummed mad riding over here, I could have rung your neck. Then when I saw you was all right, I didn't know whether to grab you and give you a hug, or kick your bottom. I done neither, just stood here dumbfounded that you was okay after pulling a stunt like that. That's all I got to say about it. It's over and done with, unless you pull something like this again. Then we're going to have us a problem!"

Janice started cleaning camp, but talked over her shoulder. "I really am grateful for all y'all are doing. I was just worried that Sam would pull this job off, and ride out of the country before I could get them. Oh, I almost forgot, nobody knows I'm a girl except y'all three. Not even Shorty knows. He thinks I'm his cousin, Jack. Let's leave it that way until this is over. Things will stay uncomplicated. If he knew I was Janice, he'd probably send me home, or at least get shot trying." She giggled out loud.

Weldon looked at Butch, then said, "well, I almost goofed twice. But what are you going to do on the robbery? I'll be tough staying out of gunfire. There'll be a lot of lead throw'd when them soldiers return fire."

"I'm going to ride along beside one of the Kraymons, preferably Sam. Then a mile or so before we hit Tecolote Creek, my horse will come up lame, or something like that. I'll tell them to go on, and I'll get off my horse and lift a hoof like he's got a stone. I'll fool around until the last rider passes me, then I'll holler at him and say I'll be along in a few minutes. I do wish y'all wouldn't worry so, I really mean it, I'll be okay."

To Janice it seemed the day would never end. She sat in the saloon watching poker games until she could tell which man was going to win by watching his actions. One man who was bald-headed, would remove his hat, and run his hand over his head, wiping away the sweat. When he did this, he always had a good hand. Another would scoot his chair back a few inches, then bring it very close to the table. When he won, he would smile and say, "By Jacks, I know'd I had y'all that time. Yes siree, I knowed it." And yet another would always take a quick shot of whiskey. She had them down pat.

Weldon was the hardest to read. He had a real poker face, never smiling. His eyes always turned to the man who was betting, before returning to his own cards. Around four in the afternoon, Janice had enough, and made the statement, "I'm bored stiff. I think I'll go on down and make camp at the same place I did last night. I'll take me a nap and be rested up for tomorrow. No telling how late we'll have to ride tomorrow night."

Butch folded his hand and pushed back his chair. "Sounds like a good idea, Ben. I think I'll drag along with you, I could use a little shut-eye myself."

Once Janice and Butch were out the door of the saloon, and walking for their horses, Janice shouted, "Why in the world would you throw down a sure winning hand just to take a afternoon nap? You didn't have to quit because of me. I was just going nuts sitting there like a bump on a log."

"Oh, yes, I did have to quit. Me or Weldon will stick right to you until this thing is completely over with. Well look yonder, here comes Roy. Sure looks as if he's been pushing his horse to the limit. Do you think he got lost, or what took him so long? Boy, he sure looks put upon, don't you think?"

Janice cringed, and whistled. "Yeah, and I'd bet it's because of me. But, you'll stick right by me and tell him everything's all right, won't you Butch? You know, you can tell him why I did it. It might help."

"Naw, let's hear him out first. He might just do a better job on you than me and Weldon did." He chuckled out loud.

"Well... I'll be a.... Thanks a lot, smarty pants! I'll remember this, just you wait and see if I don't! Just you mark my words, Mister Butch! If he kills me, you'll be sorry. Then who will you have to kick around?"

Butch was chuckling, as Roy slid his horse to a stop, inches away from the waiting pair. "Janice! If I hadn't run into Shorty, and him telling me what went on, I do believe I'd get off this horse and tan your hide! Do you hear me, Janice McCord?" In a softer voice he said, "But I'm glad you're okay. Now, where are you two headed?"

Janice smiled, "Hello, Roy. It sure is good to see you too. Me and Butch are going down along the river to camp and take us a nap. Want'a come along? You do look awfully tired." She smiled her pretty little smile.

"No! I most certainly do not want to take a nap! I'm hot and I am tired, and mentally sick from worrying about you. I'm going for a dozen or so beers, then I might feel better. Butch, Weldon is playing cards, ain't he?" Roy was shaking his head.

"Yeah, and he's doing pretty good. If you sit in with Rudd Bates and Squint Doser, you watch 'em. They're bad losers. And watch Sam too. Don't let them boys put any holes in you, or Weldon either. Just you watch 'em."

Roy turned his horse up the street, and hollered over his shoulder, "I probably won't be that long. I'm dead tired. Y'all got plenty for supper, or do I need to bring something?"

"Naw, no need of that, we got plenty. Go ahead and get your beer. We'll have supper ready in about two hours." Butch turned to Janice, saying, "Won't you, Ben?" He had an ear to ear smile on his face.

Janice laughed out loud. "Yeah, I guess that's the least I can do. I just hope it don't kill you all. I still need your help."

Shorty met the army payroll wagons about ten miles northeast of Las Vegas. When the outrider saw him coming over the horizon, he loped his horse back to the wagons. "Sergeant Mims, we got us a lone rider loping this way. Think I ought'a stop him and see what he's doing out this way?"

"No, I don't think you should stop him! This is the wagon trail, and anybody that wants can come and go as they please. We'll just call a stop and rest the horses until he comes by, and either stops or goes on his way." He hollered in a loud voice, "Bring 'em to a halt! Take a ten minute rest."

Shorty rode up in a gallop. "Howdy, Sergeant. "I'm U.S. Marshal M D Thompson. I've come to warn you about an outlaw gang that's waiting at Tecolote Creek to rob your coach. It's a pretty good sized group, and they mean business."

"And how would you have known this? Surely they are not thinking of robbing an army supply coach. The only thing they could make off with, is sugar, flour, nails and a few sets of harness. Oh, and three hundred pounds of dried beef. No, No, you must be mistaken. Outlaws wouldn't want all this."

Shorty sat with one leg around his saddle horn. "Naw, I suppose you're right, but just maybe they're interested in your fifty thousand dollar payroll for Fort Marcy. These men you have here won't last the first burst of gun fire. And to make sure, they have over fifty men." Shorty watched the Sergeant's face as it slowly went to a surprised look of confusion. He looked as if he'd been hit in the face with a cold rag.

"But, but, how could this happen? No one was suppose to know anything about this money. And it's not fifty thousand, but a little over a million dollars. General Russell assured the army that if they kept the same number of guards, we would not raise suspicions, and have no problem getting through. What would you do if you were in our place, Marshal?"

"A million dollars!" Shorty sucked wind through his teeth, and whistled long. "I now see why two of the largest, meanest gangs in the territory have joined hands in this robbery. The men only know of fifty thousand. Oh, what I'd do is move on and camp the night on the plains east of Las Vegas. Meantime I'll ride to the Fort and let the General know what y'all will be up against. You're sure going to need more men than you got here."

"Tell him I need reinforcements, and they must catch up by morning."

"Mighty good, Sergeant, I'll have word before you move in the morning. No matter what, don't go on without more men."

Shorty sat through the weirdest meeting with General Russell, he had ever been in. After an hour of discussion, no agreement had been reached as how to handle the situation. Finally Shorty stood up and started to put his hat on, but didn't. "General, why not leave the payroll in Las Vegas and fill the coach with troopers? After you wipe out the outlaws, return for the payroll."

Shorty watched as General Russell's eyes bugged out, and his face turned red. He thought he was going to die for anyone even thinking such a thing. "Marshal Thompson, the cavalry backs off from no one! The payroll will go through on schedule! There's right at a million dollars going to Fort Yuma, and must reach there in thirty days!"

"Then fill the coach with men, and let a few more bring the money along in a wagon. They could follow a couple of hours behind. After the outlaws are taken care of, you can transfer the payroll to the coach and go on. Very little time would be lost that way. Loading and unloading is all."

"Marvelous idea, Marshal! Splendid! Simply splendid thinking. If one didn't know better, one would think you were military." General Russell was beside himself, as if he were the one who came up with the idea.

Shorty smiled. "As long as it was only one person thinking it, I could just say he was crazy as a loon and out of his mind, and let it go at that."

General Russell was cleaning his spectacles, and looked over at Shorty. "As you were saying, only one person thinking what, Marshal?"

"That I was in the army. Not me, in no way, ever."

"Then you don't like the army?" Through his thick glasses, the General's eyes looked as big as the bottom of coffee mugs.

"Naw, the army's fine, it's just not for me. I've got too many places to go and too many things to do to be stuck off on some army fort someplace. And I'm not one to stand around saying, yes sir, to some hair-brained... Uh, uh saying yes sir to a bunch of orders that don't make no sense." Shorty was red.

"Sergeant West! See to a wagon at once. Put the best team in front of it and get ready to pull out. I'll have other men ready by the time you are. Get help and throw on a Gatling gun to replace those payroll boxes on top of the coach. Take along tarps to cover everything, and be sure and lash those boxes down where they won't fly loose and scatter gold along the trail."

By moon and starlight the wagon reached the mesa east of Las Vegas, just as the troops were starting to cook their breakfast. It was a pretty noisy meal, with everyone being excited about the idea of a gang of outlaws trying to rob an army payroll. Ridiculous is what it is. Boredom of slow fort life was over for awhile. Action, excitement, fighting, Shorty thought that every one of them were stupid assed nuts and told them so.

Before the sun broke the horizon, every man was through with his job. The payroll had been switched, and the Gatling gun was in its place, up top the coach. Scouts had been out for over an hour. Five out-riders led off, a hundred yards out front. Shorty was one of those. They rolled off the mesa just south of Las Vegas, and the scouts finally found a place for them to cross the Gallinas River.

Saturday morning in Villanueva was busy. Every man had cleaned his guns and taken care of his horse. Some sat in silence, while others carried on conversations about old jobs, or friends that were no longer alive. Sam was mad that his own brother would just up and ride off without telling a soul about it. Maybe Ben hadn't liked the man on boy attention, and told Nick to beat it. Sam knew Nick had himself a problem, liking little boys the way he did, but damn-it, he was a solid gun-hand.

At eight o'clock, Norm Bristol sat with Sam, eating breakfast and going over their escape route. Every soldier must be killed, leaving no one to ride to the forts for help. After the robbery they would meet at Lamy for the split. Then the gangs would ride separate ways, throwing off the swift coming, relentless, pursuit of a pissed off cavalry. Killing cavalrymen meant these men could never stop looking over their shoulder.

Norm pushed back his chair and stood up. "Sam, I think it's about time to hit the trail and get set up, don't you? We've got a lot of men to push."

"Naw, not just yet, we've got plenty of time. Besides that, I sent brother Otis, on a little trip yesterday. He ought'a be back nigh on to anytime. We'll give him another hour or so. He just might find out something we need to know." Sam looked at his watch again, and smiled to himself.

Weldon, Butch and Roy had been unsuccessful trying to talk Janice out of going. After she threw a barn kicking, stomping fit, they figured to leave her alone. Stubborn, is what she is, just plain mule headed stubborn. Somehow, between the three of them, they'd have to watch over her and keep her out of harms way. A bunch of men were about to die uselessly, too many. Some would be friends, others needed killing anyway.

Twenty minutes later just as Norm walked out to talk with his men, Otis came riding in on a horse that had been run into the ground. The horse was covered with foam and its muscles had a nervous twitch. It was staggering, trying to keep from falling down.

Otis mumbled howdies to everyone as he walked through the door, and to Sam's table. Cupping his mouth with his hand, he leaned over and whispered into Sam's ear.

Sam's eyes got big and he muttered, "Uh huh. Yeah, yeah, uh huh. And you're sure about that. Go out and get Norm."

While Otis went for Norm, Sam did some quick thinking. This could work out even better than he had ever thought, and at the same time cut down on the number of men he would have to split the loot with.

Norm walked back in and asked, "What's the hold up now, Sam? Otis is back. We're going through with it, ain't we?"

"Oh, nothing, nothing's wrong. Yeah, we're gonna do it. It's just a good thing I sent Otis out to do a little spying. The payroll is coming on with regular guards, but less than an hour back, is fifty soldiers. The cavalry must have gotten wind of this hold-up. Here's what we're going to do. You take your men and hit the payroll, then wait for us at Lamy. I'll set a little trap for them soldier boys. We'll knock them boys out'a their saddles before they have time to spit twice. Now Norm, y'all wait for us in Lamy, no matter how late we are. It'll be tough taking that many soldiers but I'm taking Weldon and his boys. If that kid with him can shoot as good with a rifle as he can with his .45, we won't have too much of a problem." Sam called for another cup of coffee, smiling inside his evil mind. "All that gold is mine!"

Outlaws were saddling horses, and hollering back and forth, with the excitement of the new job. The noise and commotion made the streets of Villanueva as busy as any mining town. Once the gangs split up and rode out, not one sound was heard in the little village. It was now back to being a weekend stop for a few cowboys, who were looking for whiskey and whores. Norm Bristol's gang headed for Tecolote Creek, where the horses would be held out of sight. The men would be well hidden, behind fallen logs and sandbars along the creek's edge. They had plenty of time to set up the perfect trap. In his mind, Norm was already thinking how he could pull this job off and cut Sam and his bunch out. He was laughing out loud. I'll just grab all that gold, and make a run for it."

Turning sideways in his saddle, Norm spoke to the man riding next to him. "Spider, this is the big one. Sam didn't tell anybody but me, but there's almost a million dollars coming in that wagon. I want you to make sure each man is in the right spot when the shooting starts. When we take this gob of loot, we're headed for Calico. Maybe even Alaska, no matter, we've got to out run Sam and his boys, and the cavalry."

Norm chuckled out loud. "That is unless him and his boys go getting theirselves killed while holding them soldiers off'n us. Mighty nice of him to do the fighting while we get the loot." He laughed out loud and put the spurs to his horse. In a very short time, Norman would be a rich, rich man.

Sam and his men rode from Villanueva in a long, hard gallop. They had several more miles to go, in less time than Norm and his men. Janice, Weldon, and Butch and Roy rode close together, bringing up the rear. Sam pulled up wide of Romeroville, riding north at the foot a high hogback ridge. Breaking from the tree line into a small clearing, Sam called everyone together.

"All right, boys, that gap is where we're hitting that payroll. I want men on both sides of the cut. Let the coach pass, it's the wagon following we want. It will be carrying the money. And dad-gum-it, don't nobody go killing the teams. We'll need them horses to pull the wagon for us. I'm telling you boys something I didn't tell Norm and his boys. There's nigh on to a million dollars in this wagon. The coach is packed pull of soldiers, and Norm will have to take care of them. I can tell everybody has questions, but talk among your selves and hold the questions for awhile. Get set, we're already late."

Butch stepped from his saddle. "Just how are we going to get a wagon all the way to Mexico, with the whole U.S. Cavalry on our tails?"

Sam rolled an eye. "It's just going to the bottom of the Gallinas River Canyon, where we bust open them boxes. Remember, stay out of sight and let that fool coach get over the hill out of sight. Otis says the wagon is a mile or so back, so don't no body go getting ants in your pants. Listen to what I have to say we'll make it. Just sit tight."

Sam and his two brothers stayed low, wanting to be the first ones to the wagon, after all the soldiers were dead. Seven of Sam's men, along with Weldon, Butch, and Roy and Janice, climbed the west side of the north ridge. Several men stayed along the bottom, low and across from Sam, while others rode to the south side and started their long hard climb to the top.

Janice looked around and punched Weldon with her elbow. She jerked her head northeast; about a mile away came the coach, with its outriders out front by a couple of hundred yards. Weldon whistled and waved his hat at Sam, who in turn did the same to the men on the south side. Everyone slid back from sight under the crest of the ridge. Janice looked up, saying, "Think I'll head back over in them bushes and do my business before they get here. When things start heating up, I might not have time."

One of the men rolled over on his elbow and said, "better you get farther away than that, kid! I don't need to be smelling you for the next hour or so. That's all the hell we need! Smelling some dumb assed, lazy kid for a couple of hours!"

Janice walked along the ridge top a couple of hundred yards until she found herself a large boulder to get behind. After relieving herself, she walked back toward the men thirty or so yards and waited. Five minutes later Weldon and Butch walked up. "What've you got on your mind, Jack? You're up to something and we know it." Weldon waited with his hands on his hips. "Better let us in on it, now."

Janice took her hat off and ran her fingers through her hair a few times. "Fellers, y'all know we can't sit by and let them bushwhack them soldiers. What do y'all think of sending Sam's men back down to him? You can tell them we can handle everything up top. When the payroll gets here, I'll start shooting Sam's men. Surely the cavalry will see what I'm doing and give me some help. Even if we don't get any help, we can take 'em, don't you think? Well, we can't let 'em do it, even if I miss one or two of the Kraymons, now."

She looked from Weldon to Butch, before saying more. "We'll have the best position. Besides that, I brought enough shells up here for all of us." Janice looked at Weldon. "This ain't very good, is it? We're in a tight spot."

Butch moved a small rock with the toe of his boot, and spoke. "I think we should just ride the heck out of here. A lot of men are about to die, and I don't want one of them being me. Weldon, what do you think? Do you think we have a chance of any kind?"

Weldon felt the beard on his chin, and looked toward the east. "It's gonna get rougher'n all get out, but Jack's right. We can't let those men be slaughtered. We have to stop it somehow. Let's think on it awhile."

Janice had her hands on her hips. "Weldon! We have run out of time! If you don't think my idea was a good one, I'll just walk on down and put a gun to Sam's head. Once I pull the trigger, it won't matter what happens to me."

Weldon took Janice by the arms, and held her for a moment. "Janice, it does matter what happens to you! You are trying to right a great wrong. You are the last McCord, and have got to stay alive. We'll do it your way, just you stay out of harms way, or I'll hog-tie you back here in these trees until its over." He released her arms and watched her face for a full minute. "Janice, I mean it now, you be careful!"

Shorty was riding beside Lieutenant Dixon, about fifty yards out front of the coach. Stopping the dun, he sat for a moment before saying, "Lieutenant, this ain't going right. Something sure is wrong, or is gonna be in a little while.

Y'all go on, but be careful of a trap. It'll be set somewhere around Tecolote Creek. If I was you, just before going over that last rise leading down to the creek, I'd put four men up under them tarps until the shooting starts. Two of them can push up the barriers while the other two fire up the Gatling gun. I'm riding back and will come on with the wagon. I sure got me this funny feeling, and it ain't very good. Them outlaws sure might try to pull a sneaky on us."

"You go ahead, Shorty, we'll be all right. Those barriers around that gun will stop any bullet they throw at us. And, the outlaws can't know anything about the Gatling. But being safe, I sure hope that feeling of yours is wrong."

Shorty turned the dun back toward Las Vegas. Janice was looking that way and saw him turn around. "Hey, Weldon, come here a minute." When Weldon got beside her, she spoke in a low voice. "Don't that look like Shorty's dun heading back toward Las Vegas? I could swear that looks like him. I'm almost sure, what do you think?"

Weldon strained his eyes, then said, "Yep, sure does. Wonder if he's going back to ride along with the wagon? Man-o-man, I sure wish he wasn't along with either bunch. I mean it Janice, in a little bit a lot of men are going to die. Money won't help the dead. All right, you go talk with Roy while I send Sam's boys down to him. They can tell Sam we sent them just in case he needed more help down low. Maybe helping to hold the spooked team." Weldon went over and started talking low to Butch.

Janice sided up to Roy and started talking about the ranch, then jerked his sleeve and told him to follow her. They walked to the top of the ridge and lay on their stomachs, watching the coach as it pulled ever closer.

Twenty minutes later the coach cleared the gap, and two hundred yards later stopped in front of the Romeroville Mercantile. Several soldiers got down and went inside. Several minutes later they came out with food and water. Sam watched as canteens and food passed through the coach windows. He openly snickered to himself as he scooted back out of sight. "I can see that gold now, and its all mine! Every damned bit of it!"

"Otis my boy, you sure was right. That coach is plumb full of soldier boys. Looks like Norm and his boys will have their hands full." He laughed softly and slapped his knee. "Darn shame they won't be alive to spend their share of loot. Yes 'tis, just a dirty rotten shame." He snickered again.

The coach pulled out of sight in a few minutes, and fifteen minutes later Weldon whistled and waved his hat at Sam. The wagon was in sight, coming on slow. Weldon spoke to Sam's men in a low, but firm voice. "This is a good vantage point. You men had better get down and help Sam. Them horses might get hard to hold, with all the shooting that is going to go on. Besides that, y'all will be there to help with the money. Just tell Sam how good our position is up here, and us four will be able to handle anything."

The men looked at each other, and greed flashed through their heads.

They crawled on hands and knees until they were below the top of the ridge. Each of them wanted to be the first one to the gold. They ran and slid down the steep hill, getting to Sam, so they could help. Little did they know, Sam didn't give a fat rat's rump about any of them. He wanted to use their guns getting the money, then if he had the chance, he would back shoot them also. He cared only for getting his hands on the gold.

Chapter Eleven

The wagon was about fifteen hundred yards from the gap, with Shorty riding point beside Sergeant Lomas. High on the bluff to the right of the cut, Shorty saw a glint of sunlight on metal. He had no idea it was Janice using the shiny barrel of her revolver to warn them. He started to pull the dun back, but hesitated for a long moment.

Janice whispered to Roy. "Did you see that? I think I saw the dun miss a step. Shorty's seen my signal, don't you think?"

"I don't know, but he could have. Just you watch his every move, and stay out of sight. I'll get over there with Weldon and Butch. Sam's gonna be mad as hell when he sees us killing his men. And we got a lot of them to kill."

Janice lay on her stomach watching, as Shorty rode back by the wagon and all the way to the drag riders. After riding along and talking for awhile, he kicked the dun into a lope. Pulling up beside Sergeant Lomas, they slowed until the wagon pulled abreast of them. Shorty raised his eyes toward the crest of the hill. Chill bumps covered his body. Something was about to happen. He hated this feeling, a whole bunch of men were about to die.

Every man started eyeing the bluff above the cut as they slowly pulled closer and closer. Even the horses started prancing, as the reins were tightened, holding them back. Shorty finally made up his mind and said, "That signal was from one of my friends that's with this bunch. That means they had a man watching when we switched the money. They just let the coach go on through, and are going to hit us here.

"I've got a friend up on the north side. The attack will come from the south bluff up high, and maybe down low from both sides. When the first shot's fired, everybody hit the ground and find cover. Nobody, and I do mean nobody, will try to fight from his horse you'd be picked off by their second volley. I figger we'll have a good two seconds to hit the ground after the first shot is fired. If my guess is right, Jack McCord will fire that first one, and it won't even come close to hitting any of us."

Weldon placed Butch and Roy where they could watch the only trail up to them. That was a hundred yards north, and above Sam's position, and wide open. There was no way anyone could get by them. Janice and Weldon had their rifles pointed toward the men who were hidden on the south bluff.

As the wagon pulled within two hundred yards of the gap, Weldon took a deep breath and said, "All right, it's time. All hell's about to break loose."

Janice took careful aim on a man who had just brought his rifle to his shoulder. "Weldon, I'm on the one wearing the red shirt. You take any of the others. I sure hate shooting anybody from ambush, but that's what they're about to do to them soldiers."

Janice's bullet hit the man about an inch under his left ear. Her next shot sat a man back down that had started to stand. The other men, including Sam and his brothers, thought the shots were at and from the cavalry. Men came from hiding to the edge of the bluff to open a barrage of shots at the wagon, they couldn't even see clearly. The men at the bottom of the bluff ran out in the open, firing wildly, in their haste to get to the gold. It was greed, not bravery that made them do this. Basically they were all cowards, and everyone of them knew it.

Shorty and the cavalry had already hit the ground and found cover. Sam's men on the south bluff had to stand and lean forward to fire down on the wagon. In doing so, they exposed themselves to Weldon's and Janice's fire. One of the soldiers lying under the wagon took a bead on someone on the north bluff. Shorty turned to see if anyone had been hit, and saw where his gun was pointed. He only had time to kick at the barrel as the rifle was fired. He hoped he kicked it in time to deflect the bullet.

"You ignorant bastard! I told you those men on the north side was friends! If you can't shoot south, don't shoot at all! Stupid shit!" Shorty wanted to kick him right in the face, and came close to doing it.

Bullets were kicking up rock shards and dirt all around the wagon. The soldiers had as good of cover as Sam's men, and didn't have to show them-selves to return fire. Sam figured by now his men had shot most of the soldiers, so him and his boys started working ever closer to the wagon full of gold. He knew nothing of his ten dead men on the south side, or that only four of them were still alive.

Unnoticed by Weldon, Janice lay unconscious ten feet away. The bullet fired by the soldier, whose gun Shorty had kicked, slammed the side of her forehead, leaving a sixteenth of an inch deep groove. It looked as if someone had started to scalp her.

Butch hollered at Weldon. "Hey Weldon, we can't see Sam and his bunch no more! They've moved out of sight into the cut."

"Y'all come on over here. Looks like only one or two are left up high, but all of Sam's ten are still alive. I counted them when they went around the bend. Janice, why don't... he looked and saw Janice, unmoving". "Janice! Oh darn! Butch! Get over here! Janice has been hit! Hurry, dang-it all to heck!" Weldon slowly lifted Janice in his arms. Blood covered her hair and face. He took off his hat and placed it under her head, lowering her limp body back to the ground. He ground his teeth together, and turned away.

Butch took his canteen and neckerchief, and began frantically washing blood and dirt from her hair, face and neck. Tears welled in his eyes, as he started rocking her back and forth.

Roy stood, shaking his head from side to side. Grabbing his rifle, he shouted, "Come on Weldon, let's finish 'em off!"

Roy and Weldon stood at the top of the bluff, firing almost straight down onto Sam and his men. One man was left alive on the south side, and saw what was going on. He took a slow, keen bead on Roy and fired.

The bullet took Roy high in the left shoulder, spinning him around and to the ground. Weldon's next shot took the gunman full in the chest.

Weldon kneeled beside Roy. Taking his neckerchief, he pressed it into the wound. "You'll make it Roy. It looks worse than it is, just hold this tight until the bleeding stops. Butch, how's Janice?"

"Alive is all I can say. I'll get over there and help you with Roy, then we'll get Janice to a doctor in Las Vegas. We gotta help her Weldon, gotta."

When they looked over the bluff, only three of Sam's men were visible, and they had their hands in the air. Shorty and the cavalry were walking forward with their guns pointed at them. They didn't seem so brave now.

Weldon kneeled beside Janice. Her breathing was shallow, and she had lost a fair amount of blood. A tear rolled down his cheek as he took off his shirt and placed it over her face. Shrieking, Butch grabbed it off, "Dang-it, don't do that, Weldon! She ain't dead, not by a long shot! Now or never!"

Butch was so shaken, tears filled his eyes, and he was screaming. "Just don't you do it again, Weldon!"

"I know she ain't dead, Butch! And she ain't gonna be. I just did that to keep the sun and flies off of her, until we can help Roy down to the horses. We'll go around and ask Shorty if we can use that army wagon to take Janice to Las Vegas. It'd be a lot easier on her. I also want to see Sam and his brothers dead!" They lifted Roy, and slowly helped him down the steep rock strewn path to the horses. Roy's bleeding had slowed, and showed signs of stopping.

Leaving Roy in the shade of a large pine tree, and beside the horses, Weldon and Butch walked into ear-shot of Shorty and the cavalry. "Shorty, don't shoot, it's me and Butch. We left Roy by the horses, he's been shot." Weldon's voice broke just a little, as he said, "and Janice has been shot in the head. It looks real bad."

Before Weldon could say another word, Shorty asked in disbelief, "Did you say Janice? I thought she was dead! Where's Jack?"

"Jack's been dead all along. Janice just passed herself off as Jack so she could get close enough to the Kraymons to kill every one of them. Hey, wait a minute! I don't see any of the Kraymon's bodies. That means Sam, Otis and Jess are still alive. Shorty, somehow the Kraymon boys got away! They must have slipped back around the hill and got their horses, while me and Butch was busy with Janice and Roy."

"Weldon, you said Janice was shot in the head, how bad is it?"

"I don't know. She's still unconscious and has lost a lot of blood. We'll need that cavalry wagon to take her back to Las Vegas to a doctor. Do you think that can be worked out?" There was hope and urgency in his voice.

Before Shorty could answer, Sergeant Lomas spoke right up. "You dad-gummed right y'all can use that wagon. If not for y'all, Kraymon would have it and all of that gold anyway. And most, if not all of my boys would be dead or hurting pretty dang bad. As far as the gold getting to Fort Yuma, it'll make it a little late, but it'll get there. We just don't have to let the General know how late it'll be." Lomas smiled right big.

Sergeant Lomas turned to his men. "You two, get these men hog-tied and ready for travel. Corporal Allen, get the wagon and take it around to wherever this man shows you. Private Horton, get the gurney ready. We'll use it to get that girl down from the bluff."

Turning to Shorty, Lomas stuck out his hand to shake. "Marshal Thompson, you and your friends saved a lot of lives today, and army money. I'll get these men's names. I'm sure the army will want to give all of them, including that girl up top, commendations of bravery. They all did an outstanding job."

Butch laughed out loud. "Sergeant, I think we'd better forego them commendations. Our names being printed up could get us hung. Until we ran into that kid lying up there, we was on the other side of the law."

"I'm sure General Russell will see to full pardons for those past deeds. If not, I will personally escort you to any location you wish to depart to, and my patrol will see to your safety. No law will apprehend you in this territory. "

The wagon was slow making its way to the bottom of the path. Roy lay where Butch and Weldon had left him. He was dead, with his throat cut, and they're horses were gone. Weldon turned pale. "Naw, naw! They went and killed Roy! Come on, let's get Janice, then I'm going after them boys. They're going to die before this day's out." Weldon was mad and wanted it to end.

Butch stood looking down at Roy's pale, bloodless face. They had been partners for several years. "Roy partner, you was a good man to ride the trails with. Best partner I ever had. It don't matter to you now, but we'll get 'em. It won't take long either."

Weldon was already up top of the bluff and started hollering his head off. "She's gone! They've gone and taken Janice with them! Oh, Lordy, Lordy, what are we going to do?" He was wringing his hands and stomping his feet, while walking in circles. "If we get close, they'll shoot her as sure as rain!" He was already descending the path, but stopped dead still and almost went to his knees. "Dear God, knowing the Kraymons, I pray they don't find out she's a girl! Those men are cruel to women, they'll use her."

Shorty walked off for a moment, with his head down. "Come on, let's bury Roy and hit the trail. They're headed north, or we'd seen them."

Butch was so mad he was trembling. "Let's get started. Sergeant, do you have a shovel we could borrow?" He kneeled and removed Roy's gun.

"Sure thing, but you men take my extra horses and get after those men. I will see to your friend here. What's his name? You know, for the marker."

Butch looked up and smiled, "Boy, I know he'll hate me for the rest of my life for this, but it's Herman. Herman Watts, age thirty-eight. Boy, he always hated that name. It was me who started calling him Roy. We laughed and joked about it for most to a year, then after awhile it seemed he really was a Roy. He may have been an outlaw, but he was a nice man. Yeah, and good."

Tears welled in his eyes, as he walked off with his head down.

The soldiers started a grave, as Shorty on his dun, and Butch and Weldon kicked their borrowed horses into a lope, headed north. They were in a shallow valley, with the hogback ridge on the east, and higher mountains to the west. Easy to follow tracks of running horses, went right down the middle.

At almost the same time this was going on, Norm and his men opened fire on the coach. This was going to be too easy. With the fall of the first soldier, the outriders dug in their heels and whipped their horses back over the ridge out of harms way.

Norm gloated and hollered at the top of his lungs. "Yee haw, watch them blue bellies run! Let's go get that gold!" Before those words were out of his mouth, a steel barrier was raised on top of the coach. By the time his men mounted and rode from cover, a Gatling gun was spitting out bullets at a speed of three hundred and fifty rounds per minute. Men and horses screamed, as bullets ripped and literally cut them to pieces. They were knocked to the ground where they kicked, trying to rise to their feet one more time. Anyone or anything that managed to stagger to his feet was shot again. The fear of man and horse was the same, the fear of knowing they were dying.

In two minutes flat the entire Bristol gang was wiped out to the last man. Three soldiers were killed, another had received a slight wound, and yet another was fatally injured when he fell from his horse while trying to dismount, and was dragged to death. Happy with their victory, the soldiers waited for the wagon in the cool shade of old cottonwood trees that grew along Tecolote Creek. The wagon of gold would be along shortly.

Chapter Twelve

They were in a long lope as Shorty glanced over at Weldon. "How long have you know'd that Jack was really Janice? And how did she get so dad-gummed good with her forty-five. She's the littlest gun totter I've ever seen. It could have been that her dad, Henry, taught her some. He was darned fast."

As they loped along, Weldon looked from Shorty to the trail ahead. "I know'd it from the second day I know'd her. First off, she wouldn't go swimming naked. Then I went and killed us a rabbit for supper, and she ate it this way." Weldon held his hands to his mouth with his little fingers sticking straight out. "I know'd it for sure right then, but kept it quiet. I ain't seen nobody better with a hand gun, and she sure can make that rifle of hers talk. Dead shot every time she pulls the trigger on any gun. I'll tell you one thing though, she can be the most contrary, stubborn, hard headed, little brat you'll ever run in to. And... and... well, right down pretty for a girl."

Shorty laughed, "Yeah, I noticed that. Too darned pretty for a boy."

He thought a minute, then added, "yeah, I'll even say she can be stubborn."

They were making good time, but could tell Sam was pushing all out. Shorty patted his dun and nudged him a little. "I'd say they're headed for Mora, or maybe Cimarron. If they get that far, there's a bunch of mining camps they can hide at. It'll be hard getting them out of there." They continued riding in silence, thinking of Janice. Would Sam find she's a girl? Maybe not, that girl is pretty smart.

When Janice regained consciousness, she was sitting with her head in her hands, fighting dizziness. Sam walked up with his gun out and cocked. He was hard faced and mad. "You've got some explaining to do, boy! But not here! Get up and come with me! As long as you don't make trouble, you'll stay alive. Y'all figgered to cut me and my brothers out of all that money. But I'll get it yet, just you wait and see."

Janice was shoved down the trail, and helped upon her horse. When mounted, Sam pushed them north. Just before reaching Montezuma, Sam saw a herd of sheep being driven toward Las Vegas. "Come on, let's split that herd. It'll cover our tracks, and we'll be on the other side of these hills. We'll spend the night back in Las Vegas, and get us a early start. We've got ourselves a lot of fast, hard riding to do. We're going to hit that payroll again, but between Santa Fe and San Ysidro. They'll never be expecting it twice."

Shorty, Weldon, and Butch rode into Montezuma, just as Sam and his brothers pulled Janice from her horse in Las Vegas. They were in the older part of town, just off the plaza. Paying an old Mexican two dollars, they put their horses in a goat shed. Going into the Liberty Hotel, they got two rooms.

"Otis, you and Jess go get us a couple of bottles and some glasses. We'll not go to the saloon tonight. Ben here is sleeping with me, and y'all will be right next door. Ben, you don't cause me no trouble, and when this is over, you just might be alive and rich. Tell you what I'm willing to do. Let by-gones be by-gones and I'll give you five thousand of that payroll. That is if you help us take it." Janice hadn't said a word. Her head hurt, and she was nauseated.

"Yeah, that's all right by me, but right now I'm hungry as all get out. I ain't eat a bite since this morning."

"Yeah, me too. Otis, y'all bring us back something to eat."

Jess and Otis left their big brother Sam to watch Janice. Janice's gun had been taken before they started their ride, so she was no threat. Sam lay back on the bed with his hands behind his head.

"Ben, boy, I figger you're too young to come up with the idea to cut me and my brothers out of all that money. Now, Butch and Roy had rode with my gang, and neither of them had the smarts to think of such a thing. Hell, Roy wouldn't even come in out of the rain, unless he was told to.

"That leaves that gambler, Weldon. Now that's a man with vision, with brains, and fast with a gun too. Deadly fast. I just never figgered he was greedy enough to try something like this. Now I am, I was going to cut Norm and his boys out of it, if I had to kill every one of 'em. I don't think I'd tried to cut Weldon out. Yep, it had to be him. When this is all over, and I have myself a new bunch of men, I'll be rich enough to send a few of the boys to bring him right to me. Maybe he'll tell me what he had in mind. Before I kill him, that is. What do you think of that? Yes sir, that's what I'll do."

"I think if he know'd 'em, they'd be dead before they got close enough to hurt. He out draw'd Pete Bristol, flat out. No contest."

Sam laughed out loud. "The heck you say! But I 'spect you're right. I sometimes forget just how smart Weldon really is. But... he's dead, no matter how long it takes."

Getting up on one elbow, he looked at Janice. "You know what I mean, kid? When I owe somebody a debt, I pay 'em off no matter what it takes." He laughed and lay back down. "I pay my debts, pay 'em off in bullets. Now that's the way to pay a debt. Yes sir, with bullets."

Sam wasn't expecting an answer, but he got one. Janice was sitting in a chair, and leaned forward, looking straight at him. "Of course you're right, Sam. I feel the same way about paying off debts, and have three more small payments to go. Can you imagine, only three more payments?" She laughed a bitter, wicked laugh.

Sam got on his elbow again and asked, "Huh, three more payments for what? What'er you talking about, kid?" Janice was staring him straight in the eyes. As brave and bad as Sam Kraymon was, a chill swept over his body. Somehow his mind registered, he was looking death right in the face.

"Oh, do I ever have a surprise for you, Sam." From her boot top came her hide-out .45. On the way up to his face it was cocked and ready to fire.

Sam made a move, but stopped dead still as Janice stood, pointing the gun so she couldn't miss, no matter which way he tried to go. Sweat seeped through the pores of his forehead. "Can you believe it Sam, Weldon told me about you always carrying a hide-out in your boot top? Well... that got me to thinking, and sure enough, it paid off. Here's what I want you to start thinking, I'm going to die at any moment. This little sucker is about to blow my head off. Then wonder if your two brothers will make it back in time to take their own bullet. But, before you die, I sure do want you to know something."

With the gun in her right hand, Janice used her left to unbutton her shirt. Opening it almost as wide as Sam's eyes, she said, "You see Sam, I'm Janice McCord, the daughter of Alice and Henry McCord! You have raped and killed for the last time! Now lay there and watch it coming, you dirt bag!"

The last thing Sam Kraymon saw were two beautiful, small breasts. As the gun exploded, a big round hole appeared in his forehead. The bullet splattered skull and brain matter all over the wall. His eyes remained wide open, showing the fear of his dying last moments. His legs jerked and flopped a few times, but with a whole that big, Janice knew he wasn't getting up.

Janice grabbed her own gun belt, before climbing out the window and running. Otis and Jess came charging into the room. Otis stood with his mouth open, staring at Sam. "It was that kid, Jess! He went and killed Sam! We've got to get him before he gets away! Come on let's head for the horses. The little son-of-a-bitch killed Sam! How in the hell could he have killed Sam? Come on Jess! Damnit, come on. He ain't fast enough to get away." They rushed into the goat shed with their guns drawn and almost scared the old Mexican to death. "Señors, what is wrong?" The old man stood with his hands held high. "I do nothing for you to kill me, Señors."

"Where's the kid? And don't lie old man! Where's he at?"

"Down the street, Señors. Toward the Gallinas River and new town. Only moments before you arrives, he jumps on his horse and rides like the wind. He looked so small, and maybe a little afraid, no?"

Otis and Jess got their horses. Mounting, they rode ever so slowly toward the Gallinas River. Otis pulled his horse to a stop. "Jess, this is stupid. This is what that kid wants us to do, foller him. Well, we're not going to. We're going to let him come to us. Let's go back and get all the money Sam has on him. That'll save us from having to hit a stage or do something else to get money. We'll be waiting for that kid, along the south road somewhere. He's got to go that way when he leaves here. He'll probably want to meet up with Weldon and Butch. You go on and get us some trail grub, I'll see to Sam.

Keep your eyes open for that kid. He could be anywhere."

Janice made the river and brought her horse to a sliding halt. Moving back along the bank, she picked a good spot and tied her horse. Grabbing her rifle she settled down beside a huge cottonwood tree. She figured to take one of them from his saddle, then worry about the other one later. Ten minutes passed, and then thirty. An hour later the disappointed Janice got her horse and started back up the street. "Stupid, ignorant, mangy men! If they wasn't so stupid, they would have followed me, so I could have shot them!"

The old man in the goat shed told her everything he knew. "Si, the men come looking, and left very angry. They are full of hate, no?"

"Yeah, they're full of hate, and when I catch them...but did you happen to see which way they went?" Janice knew they wouldn't let her get away with killing Sam. The mangy dogs must have something planned.

"Si, they ride down the street following you, at first. Then they rides back this way, and before one of them goes into the hotel, they talk for a little bit. The other one rides to the mercantile and comes out with mucho foods. When the one comes from the hotel, they mount and ride off to the south. Like maybe they are going to Romeroville, or maybe even Santa Fe. I don't know, but they were very mad hombres. Dangerous, I would say."

Janice thanked the old man, and gave him a dollar for her horse's keep. Looking at the sun, she knew it was too late to track the Kraymons today. But tomorrow she would be fresh and ready. She wondered about Weldon and Butch. Had they gotten out alive? What about Shorty, did he make it?

The old man spoke in his broken English. "If I may say so Señor, you should have your forehead looked after. It could get infected, no? You looks very pale and maybe a little sick, no? Perhaps you are weak, also."

Janice had forgotten about her wound. "Yeah, you're right. Where could I find a doctor? Is there one close?"

"Si, one block over. Just past the plaza on your left. It is Doctor Rodriquez. He is young, but a very good doctor. Please tell to him that Pepe Lopez has sent you. It is best if you don't die. You are much too young."

The doctor was very concerned about Janice. "Young man, when did this happen? You could have a concussion, as there is much swelling at your hairline. Have you not noticed, your hat does not set properly? You must have a terrible headache, no?"

"Yes, I've got a headache. This happened early this afternoon."

"You must rest with your feet higher than your head. That will help alleviate the swelling. If the swelling is not gone by morning, you could get brain damage. We must not let this happen. I will help you, but you must listen to me."

"All right Doctor, I'm yours. What do you want me to do?"

"You come with me and lie down on one of my cots. No one else is
around, so you will be able to rest. I will get wet towels for your head, and make you comfortable. You must stay very still over night. If you are hungry, my wife will bring you food."

Janice smiled, "I'm hungry all right. I ain't eat a bite since breakfast."

"My dear boy, you must not only be hungry, you must be half starved. My wife will be right in. She will bring you some of what we had for supper. Will that be all right with you? My wife is a very good cook."

"You'd better believe it. Right now I'd eat a horse that had been dead for a week. And I need a drink of water, too. For some reason I'm feeling all dried out. I'm mighty thirsty. About like a dried up creek bed."

The doctor reached and felt her forehead. "Ahhh, you also have a slight fever. We must get you the water to drink, and also a cold compress for your head. When my wife comes in, take these powders with your water."

An hour later Janice had eaten and was fast asleep. Almost at once she was dreaming. She was sitting in a beautiful blue meadow with her feet in a small stream. The same Indian girl that was in many of her dreams came and sat beside her. "Little one, do not be afraid. I am Laney Hawk, we have talked many times before. When there is much danger, I will come. I have come to warn you to be very, very careful. Do not take the normal trail south, as the two men you seek are waiting in hiding for you. They want to do you much harm. Find another path. Your journey of revenge is almost at an end, but you must ride with both eyes wide open, looking all around. You will see what you must do. These men are not wise, but are very vicious. Remember, when your path leads to happiness and truth, spirit guides will always be at your side."

Janice slept as never before. When she awoke, the swelling was gone from her forehead, and she felt great. Mrs. Rodriquez would not hear of her riding off until she ate her breakfast. "Now you listen to me young man, no matter how good you feel this morning, you need food for your strength."

Janice hadn't realized how late she had slept. It was close to eight o'clock in the morning. "Thank you for all of your help, and breakfast, but I really must hurry. I have two men waiting for me, and I know how I hate to wait on anyone." Janice knew where Otis and Jess would be waiting.

Shorty, Weldon, and Butch had stayed the night in Montezuma. At sunup they were on the road to Mora. After a couple of miles Shorty stopped the dun and dismounted. "Hey Weldon, these tracks are several days old. Sam and his brothers must have doubled back and headed for Las Vegas. You don't suppose they're headed back to Villanueva, do you? If any of Bristol's men survived, we might have a bigger problem than we do now."

"I don't know, but we've lost a lot of time. Let's kick these horses out and see if we can catch them in Las Vegas. If they hit a saloon, we'll get 'em."

Less than a half-hour before Shorty, Weldon and Butch rode into Las Vegas, Janice took the road to Romeroville. Two miles south of town she turned her horse west. After going through a shallow, narrow canyon, she turned back south. Now she was on the Montezuma trail that Sam had dragged her north on the day before. She knew beyond a doubt that Otis and Jess would be on the same ridge she had been on. That was the best location for an ambush, and she wasn't going to fall for it. "Men are really stupid!"

When they were through with breakfast, Shorty asked, "Weldon, we all know what Janice's horse looks like, but did y'all happen to know what Sam and his brothers are riding? I wasn't around them enough to know."

Weldon smiled. "Yeah, we sure do. Let's head for old town." Crossing the Gallinas River, they rode slowly up the street. Weldon jerked his horse to a stop in front of the undertaker's parlor. Sam was all laid out in a new coffin, leaned against the wall.

"Oh boy! Janice is on the loose. She's already got Sam. We'd better find out which way she went chasing Otis and Jess. And we were worried! Ha! She gets in and out of trouble quicker than anybody I've ever knowed."

"Si, Señor, I know of the small boy of whom you speak." The old Mexican was nervous of all gringos. "He is a little hombre, no, but he shoots that man at the undertakers right between the eyes, then goes to the doctor to have his head fixed. He had a big, bad lump at his hairline and stayed at the doctor's all night. Maybe an hour or so ago, he gets his horse and says two men would be waiting for him on the trail. Which trail, he did not say. He did not tell me this. But he looked brave, and rode off in a hurry."

"Thanks, Mister. We'll ride south, maybe we'll have some luck and find him." Shorty mounted his dun saying, "Let's hook 'em fellers. No telling how far we'll have to ride today. Y'all wouldn't figger she was talking about that same hogback ridge at Romeroville, that y'all was on, do you? Surely they could find a better place than that to ambush one tiny girl."

They were in a long lope as Weldon said, "Yeah, knowing Jess and Otis, that's where they'd be. I wonder how she knows they'll be waiting for her there? Dad gumit! I'll bet Janice does know that, and is headed there right now. Come on, let's kick these horses out just a might, she'll need help with them two. With Sam dead, them two will be like cornered rattlers."

They had their horses in a run when they passed the cut off Janice had taken up the canyon. Butch brought his horse to a sliding stop on its hind legs. "Hey Shorty, Weldon, hold up a minute! I need to look at these sets of tracks. A horse cut right here and was throwing dirt clods. It was in one heck of a hurry." Butch dismounted and kneeled beside the tracks. "Yep, just as I thought. These tracks belong to Janice's horse. She's going to ride up behind Jess and Otis. She'd better watch herself, them two are sneaky son-of-a guns. I'd bet she's riding into a trap."

Shorty rode up the canyon first, followed by Weldon, then Butch. The canyon was narrow and hard to traverse, and following horse tracks on rock caused them to lose a little time. Once through the canyon, Janice's trail was easy to see as they turned south.

Janice had dismounted several hundred yards down a hidden trail, and tied her horse out of sight. Walking and running low, she made her way along the ridge from the north end. She knew Jess and Otis wouldn't be watching this unseen trail. It took her ten minutes to reach the relatively flat top of the ridge. Walking easy from rock to rock, and tree to tree, she spotted Jess squatting over a smokeless fire making coffee. Otis seemed rolled up asleep.

Janice waited until she was only fifty feet away when she spoke. "Jess, don't move, I've got you covered. Wake Otis and let's go for a little ride. You fellers will hang for the rape and murder of Alice McCord, and the murders of her husband and my twin. It's taken me months, but you two will hang. Marshal Thompson should be in Las Vegas about now. He'll handle you two."

Jess only lifted his eyes as he watched Janice walk closer. He reached over and poured himself a cup of coffee, saying, "You'd best sit down, kid, and talk this over. No sense going off half-cocked. Wadn't no witnesses left alive at the McCord place. Sam and Ed made sure of that. We knew what we was suppose to do before we ever got there. We was to kill McCord hisself, and the two kids, then take the woman any way we wanted to. Only one kid was home, and Sam shot him right in the face. I'll tell you what, when we find Nick, he'll tell you the same thing I just did. Here, want a cup, it's good'n hot? Or are you too damn young to drink coffee?"

"No! I don't want a cup, and you're not going to find Ed or Nick! I killed them just like I did Sam! If either of you move, I'll have the excuse to kill you. Now get up from there and get Otis, we're headed back to Las Vegas."

"Don't turn around, kid, or I'll blow your backbone plumb through your belly button! Drop that rifle and stand right still like." Otis was on his belly, and behind a low rock. Janice couldn't tell where his voice was coming from, or she would have turned and fired. She knew Otis hadn't moved since he started talking, so he had to have good cover. She slowly lowered her rifle to the ground, then stood with her fists clinched tight.

"Jess, get his pistol, and careful, we don't want him getting brave and me having to kill him before we get some answers." When Jess had Janice's pistol, Otis got up and walked around in front of her. "Thought you was pretty smart coming up that unused trail, didn't you kid? Well, I spotted it when me and Jess was coming back this way. We worked out our little plan; me being asleep, and Jess making coffee. Now you're going to tell us more about how you killed our brothers, Ed and Nick. And how'd you get the drop on Sam? We wadn't gone more'n ten minutes."

Janice stood defiant. "Give me back my .45, and I'll show you how I got Sam. He was laying on the bed, and handed me my .45, and asked if I really knew what to do with it. I showed him I knew exactly what to do. I shot him between the murdering eyeballs. As for as Ed, I beat him to the draw so bad, I could have waited a full minute before I pulled the trigger. If you ever see Billy the Kid, ask him, he saw it. Nick was just plain stupid, he liked little boys and wanted me to sleep with him. I shot him and he fell in the Pecos River.

"Y'all five Kraymons killed three of the McCord family. I feel pretty dad-gummed good getting three of y'all. At least it's now one for one. When y'all kill me, my cousin, U.S. Marshal Shorty Thompson, and Weldon and Butch, will kill you two. Then that will make five dead Kraymons, and four dead McCords. We'll be one up on you. Marshal Shorty is on your trail right now. In a day or so there won't be any more McCords, or Kraymons. You five brothers saw to that when you decided to kill my family. Dirty rotten mangy coyotes, is what all of you are! You're the lowest scum that ever walked, killing innocent people!"

The more Jess listened to Janice, the madder got. "Kill the little skunk, Otis! Blow his rotten damn'd head off! Do it, Otis! Right now, or I will!"

"Hold on, Jess! Now hold on just a damn minute. What if the kid ain't lying, and he does have a U.S. Marshal for a cousin? Now we know Weldon and Butch are riding with him, Roy was. Before you slit Roy's throat, did he say anything about maybe a U.S. Marshal riding with them?"

"Naw, he just grunted and told me to go to hell. That's when I opened him up. Now don't you stand there and let this kid talk you out of killing him! Dang it all to heck, Otis, you're making me mad! Really mad! Kill him!"

Janice screamed, "Let him do it Otis! That's the way he killed my family and poor Roy. When someone is helpless, Jess feels brave and deadly!"

"Now you shut your trap, kid! Don't piss him off any more! Damn it, Jess! I'm thinking! I'm thinking! Just you hold your damned horses a minute! I told you I'm thinking! Now pour me a cup of coffee and let me think this out."

Jess never took his eyes off Janice as he poured himself and Otis a cup of coffee. Setting his cup down, Jess took a pigging string and tied Janice's hands behind her back. "Sit down, kid, and keep your mouth shut!"

Jess got his coffee and sit down beside Otis. "What'er you thinking we ought'a do, Otis? Surely you're not thinking of not killing this little vermin. He's killed three of our brothers, and wanted to turn us in to hang. Let me kill him. Come on Otis, let me do it right now, huh Otis, can I?"

"No, not yet. Lets get camp picked up, we gotta ride. I don't know how much time we have. That Marshal, along with Weldon and Butch could be tracking him right now. We can't take the chance and kill him now, when we might have to use him to save our lives." Otis was beginning to believe everything Janice had said, and was worried. He sent Jess to get Janice's horse, and check their back trail.

After tying Janice's hands to her saddle horn, Otis helped Jess pick up the rest of their gear. Fifteen minutes later they rode toward Anton Chico. Jess hollered over at Otis, "Where are we headed, Otis? Why not toward Santa Fe? You always said you liked Santa Fe, remember? I know, we're back tracking, huh? Throwing them off our trail's what we're doing, huh Otis?"

"I don't know Jess, but we can't hang around these parts. Once Weldon and Butch put out the word about what we went and done to them McCords, and old Roy, we'd be in a heap of trouble. Even the owl-hoot trail won't be safe for us." Otis was quickly beginning to grasp their situation.

"Then let's ride Otis, ride until you say stop."

"Yeah, and if need be, we'll hold a gun to this kid's head and make 'em back off. He's our guarantee of getting out of this country alive."

Jess smiled. "Oh, now I know why you wouldn't let me kill him. I think you're as smart as Sam ever was. You know, we've still got friends in Fort Sumner, and White Oaks. Huh, Otis? Prob'ly even Lincoln too."

Weldon waited at the bottom of the trail, beside two piles of fresh horse droppings. Butch climbed the ridge to see if Otis and Jess had been there. Shorty rode on over to the mercantile to ask questions of anyone he saw. He waved to a sheep herder and stopped to talk. Someone had to see something.

"Si, Señor, it was two men and one small boy with his hands tied to the saddle horn. They were going toward Anton Chico. That is all I know. The boy didn't look happy."

"Thanks, feller." Shorty saw Weldon and Butch riding up, and waited.

"Shorty, Butch found some red hot coals, and believes he spotted Janice's foot prints. At least they could have been fresh. "

"Yeah, that had to be them. This feller here said that two men, and a small boy with his hands tied, rode past here a little over an hour ago. It looks like Janice got herself back into trouble after all. From looking at those horse droppings back there, I'd say they're on rested horses, and we're not. We may be a good while catching them, but let's ride."

Weldon pulled back on his reins. "Hold up, Shorty. How much trail grub do you have? Me and Butch are just about out, no more'n enough for a couple of meals. If we're in for the long haul, we're gonna get all mighty hungry." Weldon didn't like going without food, if it could be helped.

"Yeah, you're right. Why don't you and me get what grub we'll need, while Butch waters the horses and fills our canteens? It'd sure save time."

"Yeah, and we could be running out of time. No telling what them two have in mind, and by now, they may know that she's a girl. Let's hurry and hit the trail. I just hope our horses hold out."

Shorty looked his dun over, saying, "Dunnie will make it, but I'm not going to over push him. Ruining a horse ain't going to help Janice."

By the time Otis, Jess and Janice, left the pine covered mountains, and pushed their horses across tall grass lands to the Pecos River, the horses were lathered and blowing hard. Janice watched as both men let their horses bury their muzzles deep into the swift running water. She held her horse back and started to say something, but thought better of it and kept her mouth shut. "Those poor horses will founder within the hour."

Otis looked over at Janice, saying, "Boy, what'er mumbling about? You'd better let that horse drink. It's a long way to next water."

Janice had a stern tone to her voice. "It won't matter how far it is if we don't rest these horses now! Not a one of them will make another ten miles."

Jess looked at his horse. "Maybe he's right, Otis. This'n is pretty weak. I thought I felt him stagger a time or two. He's drunk all he can, and is still trembling something fierce. Won't hurt none to rest a bit, us too. I never seen nobody on our back trail, when I went and picked up his horse."

"Yeah, you're right. We'll rest a half-hour or so. Maybe these horses will eat a little grass. That could help cool them off."

As soon as Janice's hands were untied, she dismounted and started removing her saddle. Otis jumped over and grabbed her by the arm. "Just what in the hell do you think you're doing, kid? We ain't going to be here long enough for that. We just want these horses to rest and cool down."

Janice gave him a stupid look. "Do you want them to cool down in half an hour, or do you want it to take all day. By removing the saddles, the heat will leave through their backs, as well as their chest and stomachs. How long have you been riding a horse, any way? Saddles will hold in the heat."

"I've been riding a good sight longer than you have, smart aleck little shit! But you're right, we'll unsaddle 'em. They will cool off quicker."

Janice lifted her hands to Otis. Don't retie me, I need to get me a drink of water, and I ain't going to try to run off. My horse is unsaddled and you have my gun. I'm going to sit on the river bank and rest."

Otis looked her in the eyes. "Kid, you try something, and you're dead! Marshal for a cousin, or not. You're dead, you got that?"

"Yeah, yeah, I got it." She figured she was anyway, when they wanted.

Janice kneeled on the riverbank, cupping her hands and drinking slowly. The river looked deep and swift at this point. She glanced down stream to see how far it was to the first bend. It looked to be maybe a hundred and fifty yards. Under her breath, she said to herself, "Jack, I sure hope you taught me how to swim well enough in the Rio Hondo, to make that first bend under water. But still, I'd rather drown than be shot by these two."

Sitting with her legs folded, she started talking to Jess. "Jess, why did all the Kraymons turn out so dad-gummed rotten? You know, killing innocent people that had never done y'all no harm. Yep, a pretty sorry, rotten bunch as far as I'm concerned. Wonder if your folks would have been proud of you?"

Janice knew she was making him as mad as hell.

"Otis, if you won't let me kill him, let me hurt him just a little! Please!"

Otis moved and started to say something, but Janice jumped, shouting, "Wonder who them riders are that's coming this way?" She pointed north.

Otis and Jess jumped to their feet. Janice stood with her arm pointing, then turned and dived into the river. Both men heard the splash and turned at the same time. Janice's legs were just slipping out of sight, under the rushing water. Jess pulled his gun and started to fire, but Otis stopped him.

"No need of that, Jess. That river's to fast and deep for anybody to be able to swim in it. He's already dead. Nobodies coming, guess he just wanted to drown hisself instead of taking a bullet. Saddle up, and let's get moving. We'll leave his horse ground tied, maybe it'll slow anybody down that's looking for him. We gotta ride hard, now. We can't let 'em catch us. We don't have any cover." As they mounted, Otis looked back to the north, knowing someone was already on their trail. He could see no one, he just felt that he and Jess were in deep trouble.

Chapter Thirteen

Janice held her breath until she thought her lungs would burst. She shot to the top of the water, desperately needing air. Taking in deep gulps, she looked around. The river had pushed her so far down stream, she was unable to see where she had dived in. As a matter of fact, she had gone so far under water, the bend she wanted to hide behind was several hundred yards back up river. She quickly swam to the bank, and pulled herself, dripping and shivering from the cold water.

"Shoot fire! Either I'm a better swimmer than I thought, or the river is swifter. Lying on the bank to rest a moment, she looked back west along the river's edge. Getting to her feet, she walked slowly for a couple of minutes, then stopped and sat down. Removing her boots, she emptied them of water and looked at her forty-five.

"Man-o-man, am I ever glad Weldon told me about Sam carrying a hide-out in his boot. Heck of an idea, I'd never thought of it on my own, and that's probably because I'm not a rotten person, yet. Ha, ha." She laughed out loud, then got real quite.

"Now, I sure hope Jess and Otis have stopped looking for me, and have gone on. It'll give me time to get my thoughts about me before I take up their trail again. Boy, are they ever going to be surprised. Me, a bad penny! Ha!"

Two hundred yards farther up stream, Janice saw her horse with her head lowered, eating grass. Otis and Jess were nowhere around. "Dang, I wonder why they didn't take my horse? She's sure as heck better than either of their buzzard baits. It couldn't have been because they're not horse thieves." She laughed to herself. "Not horse thieves! They're murdering horse dung! They'd steal their own mother's eye-balls if she wasn't looking. But...just wait until I see them again."

Janice walked up and slapped her horse on the rump. "Ready to go, big girl? We ought'a catch them in about five or six miles with two dead horses at their feet. If we're lucky, it'll be less than that."

She went through her saddlebags for dry shells. Kicking the wet ones from her forty-five, she had a satisfied look on her face as she shoved fresh cartridges in their place. "Now let me see one of them no good coyotes."

She threw the saddle on her horse and was cinching it up when she heard riders coming from the north. Shorty was in the lead, followed by Weldon and Butch. Shorty brought his dun to a sliding halt a few feet away from her. "Janice! You're all right! Boy, you sure had us worried. An old Mexican sheep herder said you left Romeroville with your hands tied to a saddle horn, and didn't look to happy about it."

"Yeah, Otis and Jess skunked me and had me for a little while. But... when I went swimming in the Pecos, they wouldn't follow. Afraid of water, I guess." She laughed. "And boy was that water ever cold and swift."

Before Janice could say another word, Butch cut in. "Kind'a always thought you was all wet. Now, do you know if they're still headed south?"

"Yeah, they're headed for Fort Sumner, but we don't have to hurry. When we got here, their horses buried their muzzles in the river for at least five minutes. They won't get a good five miles before them horses quit. Shorty, I'm sorry about having to fool you into thinking I was Jack, but that's the only way I could work around men with a gun."

All the men had dismounted, letting their horses blow a bit. "I can see why you did it, but why didn't you send for me sooner? You know, the law's better equipped to handle owl-hoots like the Kraymon bunch."

Janice smiled her crooked little smile. "I don't know, but I think me and this forty-five have done pretty well. After all, I've already got three of them, and if y'all would leave me alone, I'd have the other two before dark."

Shorty tightened the cinch and stepped into the saddle. "All right, these horses have rested enough. We've got the last two Kraymons to catch."

Kicking their horses into a fast lope, they covered ground in a hurry. Less then an hour later, off in the distance, they saw two men standing beside their downed horses. Slowing to a walk, Janice reached and lifted her .45 just a bit. Now it sat a little lighter in the holster. They were still over three hundred yards away when the two men started shouting and waving their hats. Weldon stood in his stirrups and said, "Wonder why they'd do that, knowing we was coming? Of course, I've know'd a lot brighter men than any of the Kraymons. Especially these two Kraymons."

Janice was standing tall in her saddle. "Because them two fellers ain't Jess and Otis. They're way too young, and not big enough. They're just two darn kids. Come on, let's go!" She kicked her horse into a run.

Sliding to a stop, Janice sat with her hands on the saddle horn. The cowboy's didn't know whether to be thankful, or scared. Weldon and Butch rode up beside Shorty and Janice. Shorty finally asked, "What happened?"

"Man, are we ever glad to see y'all. We saw two men coming our way on horseback, and the horses looked to be staggering a lot and about ready to fall down. We rode over to see if we could help, and they draw'd their guns on us. Before we knew what was going on, they rode off on our horses, and left us these. It wasn't more than a few minutes when they dropped and died. Think you fellers could give us a lift back to Anton Chico?" They looked sad, and hopeful. "We'd be obliged "

Weldon asked Shorty, "Think you and Janice can handle Jess and Otis? If you can, me and Butch will give these fellers a lift back to Anton Chico. We'll have to ride double, so it'll take us a good while. If we don't stove up a horse, or have any problems, we'll only be a couple hours behind y'all."

Before Shorty could answer, one of the young cowboys spoke up. "Janice! Do you mean to tell me, he's a girl?"

Butch laughed out loud. "Yeah, and a right down pretty one, don't you think?" Butch watched both the young men's faces.

"Well, yeah, sure, I guess so. But I ain't never seen that short'a hair on a girl before, that's all. And a gun totter to-boot. Kind'a young for that."

Shorty smiled. "Weldon, you and Butch go ahead and help these fellers. Me and Janice will trail Jess and Otis." Asking the young men, "How fresh was y'all's horses?"

"Good'n fresh. We'd only come about twenty miles, and hadn't choused 'em at all. We was on our way to the fiesta over at Las Vegas. There sure is a lot of pretty little señoritas that love to dance."

Butch asked, "If you was going to Las Vegas, what good will Anton Chico do? Vegas is still better'n another thirty miles."

"We'll get horses from Mister Garcia. He knows us real good, and he's a cousin to our ramrod. We'll still make the fiesta."

They split up, with Weldon and Butch taking the boys north by northwest. Shorty and Janice headed for Fort Sumner. Pushing their horses hard and long. The high grass- lands were easy on the horse's hooves. They didn't have to worry about Jess and Otis waiting in hiding to jump them. The hills were long and rolling, and bare of vegetation, except for long stemmed grass. They were making good time, but still had to night camp about forty miles short of Fort Sumner. "Shorty, if only it was a full moon, I'd ride all night." Janice smiled.

By not eating breakfast, and breaking camp at first light, they arrived in Fort Sumner a little after ten o'clock. Putting their horses in the livery, and seeing they were taken care of, their next stop was a cafe. They both were starving. After a good hot breakfast, they hit the first saloon.

Shorty drank a beer, and Janice had a sarsaparilla. They asked the bartender if he'd seen either of the Kraymon brothers. "Yep, shor did. A bit earlier though. Two of 'em stopped by and had one beer for breakfast, then took a couple bottles of rot gut with them when they left. Over heard 'em saying something about White Oaks, and Lincoln. I believe Otis even mentioned Tombstone." The bartender lowered his voice and leaned forward. "Looked to be running, they'd left their horses tied at the hitch rail."

"Thanks, we've got to wait for some friends." Shorty smiled.

"Take as long as you want, Shorty. I'm going to take me a hot bath and then a nap. Sleeping out on the ground every night is making me feel old, I guess. I didn't sleep well, I'm plumb tuckered out." Janice started to walk off.

Shorty laughed out loud. "Yeah, I noticed that right away. You sure do look old and your wrinkles are showing. Now you go on and get your much, needed rest. Where'll you be? The hotel or the livery?"

"The hotel, and thanks a lot!" Janice stomped off in a huff, as Shorty saw an early morning card game, and asked if he could sit in.

After her hot bath, Janice was asleep in fifteen minutes, and didn't awake until one in the afternoon.

Weldon and Butch walked in as Shorty and Janice were eating. Weldon pulled out a chair and sat down. "No luck, huh? By the way, do y'all always eat in the middle of the afternoon?"

Shorty took a sip of coffee and said, "Now and again. And we did have a little luck. At least we know which way they went."

Talking through their late lunch, Butch looked over at Janice. "Well now, if we don't look like a fresh picked daisy this afternoon. Bathed clean, hair brushed, and a pinched cheek here and there. Are you trying to turn girl on us old boys? Come on now, tell it true."

Janice jumped up and gave him a stare that would have stopped the sun from shining. With both hands on her hips, "I am a girl!"

Half an hour later they were in a long fast lope, on the trail to White Oaks. Janice rode in silence, knowing the end of the Kraymons was growing near. As she through of her parents, and Jack, a tear rolled down her cheek. All of a sudden she felt all alone and scared. How could a fifteen-year old girl run a ranch the size of Whip Cord? Where would she ever find ranch hands that would work for anyone so young, much less a girl? Half out loud she said to her self, "I'll do it anyway! Even if it's by myself! Stupid men!"

Weldon heard her mumbling and asked, "Can't you share your problems with friends? Maybe we can help."

She looked up, embarrassed that anyone had been looking at her and saw the tear, or heard what she said. "Oh, no, Weldon, it's nothing. I don't have any problems. I was just rambling on to myself. Everything will work out for the best, just wait and see. It always does. I have someone to help me when I get scared, or in a bind. She'll help, she's all I need. Every time before she's helped me out."

In White Oaks they found that Otis and Jess had eaten in the cafe and watered their horses before taking a seldom-used trail over the mountains toward Lincoln. It looks like they were going to Lincoln as previously thought, or did they have something more devious in mind? Why hadn't they stayed to the main road? This could mean more trouble, and everyone knew it.

Janice got all wide-eyed and nervous. "You don't think we'll lose them, do you? I knew I should have stayed on their trail myself!" The three men looked at one another, and as one said, "Yeah, we sure could lose them if they know this country pretty well. They must know by now that we're after them." Shorty swore to himself. "How stupid can I get?"

They hit their horses in a run. This would be a long hard ride. They nor the horses would get a rest until they rode into Lincoln. They had to try and cut them off. Janice kept up the lead as they cut through tall timber and rock outcroppings. This short cut would be quicker, but harder on the horses.

Hours later they topped the north mountain before riding down into Lincoln. Looking down main street, very few horses were to be seen. Why? This time of day, business should be booming. Slowly they rode down the middle of the street. A face or shadow would appear in a doorway, or window, then disappear as the riders got closer.

Shorty called a halt, and they sat still, looking from one end of town to the other. No noise was to be heard. No blacksmith hammer; no clanking of glasses from the saloon; and no children running and playing. "Weldon, you and Butch grab Janice and get the hell out of here! Six or seven guns are pointed straight at us. Don't look, but three are up and around the hotel, and a couple more at the livery. Just turn and ride like hell. Go! Hit 'em hard! Someone is about to blow the hell out of us!"

As their horses hit full stride, bullets hit the ground all around them. Everyone lay low over their saddle horns and headed off main street and raced through the trees. Weldon and Butch pulled their rifles from their scabbards as they left their running horses. Janice was still riding, circling to the south and west. She had thoughts of her own.

Butch found his first target, and watched as his bullet dropped him from a windmill tower. Looking over, he asked Weldon, "What in the hell did we ride into? This couldn't be Jess and Otis! Did you see which way Shorty went? And where in the hell is Janice?"

Weldon hadn't fired a shot, but had a worried look on his face. "Butch, I don't like the looks of this. Did you see a badge on that feller's shirt as he fell? If my eyes ain't gone plumb bad, that feller hiding behind the hotel sign has one on him. But why in the hell would the law start shooting at us? You hadn't killed anybody around here, have you?"

Shorty and Janice had circled town, and came riding in from the west. Both had their guns blazing. Shorty dropped two men from above the saloon, and Janice shot two from the hotel balcony. Ten or more shots were fired at them as they rushed past Weldon and Butch,s location.

Weldon whistled and waited for them to get back to him and Butch. "Shorty, what in the hell's going on? If I'm seeing it right, those old boys are wearing badges. Did y'all see any on the ones you shot?"

"Badges! Hell no, we didn't see any badges! What in the hell would the law be doing shooting at us? This is Garrett's town. Okay, y'all take Janice and move back where you can stay out of range of their guns. I'm going to hot foot it around and go in the back of Garrett's jail. Something is damn sure wrong, and I'm going to find out what! Y'all watch after my dun."

Shorty took his time snaking around to the back of the jail house. Putting his ear close to the door, he listened for a good two minutes. Not a damn sound was heard. Slowly he tried the door latch, but the door was locked. Peeking around the side of the building, he inched his way toward the street. Just as he approached the cell window, he heard a cough.

Looking around he saw a wooden rain barrel. Rolling it under the window, he grabbed hold of the bars. Standing on tiptoes, he could see inside the cell. Pat Garrett was lying on a bunk, with a bandage around his skull, and the cell door was closed. "Pssst, hey Pat. It's me, Shorty." Pat never moved, nor did he answer. Shorty got down and picked up several small pebbles. Climbing back on the barrel, he tossed one at a time through the window, until one hit Pat in the face.

Pat slowly opened his eyes, and quickly brought one finger to his lips. Swinging his legs to the floor, he sat up for a moment and listened. Standing, he leaned over where he could see the door though the bars. Shorty started to say something, but Pat brought his finger back to his lips, fast. Fumbling around in his shirt pocket, he found a stub of a pencil, and a small scrap of paper. As Pat started writing, Shorty heard a sound behind him and dropped from the barrel. His gun was in his hand in the blink of an eye.

There stood Janice, with her gun in her hand. Through clinched teeth, Shorty hissed, "Damnit! Don't ever sneak up on a man that way! It'll get you killed! What in the hell are you doing back here, noway?"

Whispering, she let him know she didn't like being yelled at. "I just came to see if I could help! We're up against about a dozen more lawmen. I seen their badges, and heard 'em talk. They're supposed to kill all of us, including you. No way are you to leave this town alive."

"The hell you say! Where'd you find out all of this?"

"I snuck around and when two of them went to the outhouse, I got close and listened to what they was saying. I think they know that you are Shorty Thompson. They were asking each other if he had shot a US Marshal, yet."

"Boy howdy, I wonder what in the hell we rode into?"

Pat thumped the bars, and Shorty turned as a note dropped to the ground. He couldn't believe what he was reading. 'Santa Fe Cartel, Regulators! Taking over every township! Jess and Otis Kraymon was here and talked with them. Regulators knew you were coming. Go to Fort Stanton for U.S. Cavalry. My only chance. Hanging me tomorrow morning.'

Shorty turned toward the cell window to say something, but changed his mind. "Janice, lets go. We got big problems." Watching their backs, they ran into the woods, and around to where Weldon and Butch were waiting. Shorty raised his voice, "why in the hell did you let Janice follow me? It liked to have got her shot!" He sat down on a log, and wiped the sweat from his brow.

"This shit has got to stop!"

Butch bowed up. "We! Let her! Shorty, you know damn good and well she does what she wants to! She's like a bull in a china closet. What she don't break, she shits on. Now, who do we have gunning for us?"

Weldon was cleaning his guns, and listening. He had an old feeling, he shouldn't even be in this country. All hell was about to break loose.

Shorty lifted his eyes toward town, and started to talk. It's the Santa Fe Cartel we're up against. They've got Pat locked in his own jail, and he said he was to be hung come morning. Do any of y'all want to help me wipe these bastards out? If you don't want to, I'll understand. But damn, Pat needs us."

Janice was standing next to her horse. "Shorty, what did he say about Jess and Otis? I saw some of that note. They're why we was fired on, ain't it?"

"Yeah, they are. They've already cut and run. Pat wants us to go after the cavalry, but I don't think we've got that much time. Weldon, Butch, I need to know if you're up to it. If not, I'm still going it alone."

Weldon was filling the cylinder of his .44, and flipped it shut. "Shorty, just what in the hell is this Santa Fe Cartel, noway? I've never heard of it."

"It's a outlaw group that our Lieutenant Governor set up so he can steal land and cattle from the small ranchers. I think the little Mexican shit is trying to declare Marshal Law. He knows honest lawmen like Pat Garrett won't put up with his deals, and killings. Somebody told him about me, a U.S. Marshal coming this way. My guess is it was Jess and Otis. Better than half of his regulators did at one time, ride with the Kraymons and Bristols. This was several years ago. Anyway, his Marshal Law don't mean dittly squat to a U. S. Marshal, and he knows it. He's just a little murdering bastard!"

Butch got a long face and said, "Well, damnit, if you think we can take these bastards, then lets get to it. Jess and Otis are getting farther away."

"Weldon, Janice, are y'all in on this? If you are, we'll get all set up, and hit them right after dark. No matter where they're at, they'll have light so we can see them right good. I think the four of us are as good as the twenty or so we'll be up against. We gotta work it right, but it will work."

Weldon stood and holstered his .44. "Well, Shorty, are you going to tell us what you've got in mind, or are you keeping it a secret?"

"Oh yeah, we won't have any trouble at all. Being as Butch probably knows half of them, he can just ride in and find out where everybody is at. Then he can come back and tell us, where we'll all four stay together and go get 'em. How does that sound? Butch?" Shorty half smiled.

"Sounds like y'all won't have any trouble at all. But what if Jess and Otis told them I'm now riding with you? I may have to shoot my way out."

Janice walked over and put her hand on his shoulder. "Butch, don't go getting yourself in a bind. I'll go in. Nobody would suspect me of anything. I look too young. Shorty, maybe it'd be best if I did go first."

"You may be right. But you listen to me, and I mean good! Don't go asking a bunch of stupid questions. Just find out everyone's location. I know most of them will be in the saloon, but some will also be at the jail. Its five o'clock now, it'll be dark in a couple more hours. You'd better ride all the way north and come into town from the northwest. And, I believe it'd be best if you took off your gun-belt." He watched Janice's face.

Janice put her hands on her hips and started to blow up, but said, "Yeah, I guess you're right. I'll just put it in my saddle bags."

Janice rode in from the northwest, and got all the way in front of the hotel before two men walked out in the street. They held their hands up for her to stop. "All right, Kid, where do you think you're going?"

Janice's eyes were as big as she could make them. "Just to the mercantile for some jerky, then by the saloon for my sarsaparilla. That's all."

The man who had said nothing, rasped out, "Hell fire, Clyde, let the kid go! Next thing you know, you'll be stopping old women! You already know our orders, and this ain't one of 'em!" He turned and walked back to the hotel porch, mad that Clyde had made him walk out into the hot street.

Clyde slapped the sorrel on the shoulder. "Go ahead, kid."

Janice tied up in front of the mercantile. Taking in the whole town with a glance, she went inside. Mrs. McSweeney was sitting in a rocker, fanning herself. "Afternoon, young fellow. Need something? Wait a minute, I know you. You were in a few weeks ago and got five pounds of jerky. Is that what you're after now?" Mrs. McSweeney hadn't gotten to her feet.

Janice walked back beside her chair, and in a low voice asked, "Is anyone else here?" She had been looking all around.

"No, no one else is here. Is something wrong? Why are you whispering? Do you know something about my husband?"

"No Ma'am. I just thought you might know what's going on around town. You know, like Sheriff Garrett being locked up in his own jail."

"Sheee, don't talk so loud! Of course I know what's going on! It's that dumb Lieutenant Governor. He's sent men down here to take over most of this ranching country. It's a farce about all of this being an old Spanish land grant. If Governor Lou Wallace knew what was going on, there would be a change of Lieutenant Governors. This one would be in jail, with a lot of his friends."

Janice kneeled down on one knee, beside the rocker. "Mrs. McSweeney, U. S. Marshal Shorty Thompson, and two of my friends are waiting for me out in the woods. I came into town to find out where everyone is, then I'm going back. Then we'll ride in here and take them. How many are they?"

"To start with, only eighteen, but someone rode in a little while ago, and killed five of them. Four more of them are wounded. All of them are in the saloon, on the bottom floor of the hotel. No, I take that back. Two are at the jail, making sure Sheriff Garrett doesn't get loose. They want to hang him."

Janice patted her on the hand. "Thanks, you've been a great help. When you hear shooting, hit the floor, or at least move to a back room."

Janice pitched a nickel on the counter, and took four pieces of jerky. She sauntered out to her horse and took her time mounting. Turning the horse, she rode slowly up the middle of the street, and out of town, heading northwest.

Shorty, Weldon, and Butch were all ears when Janice told them what Mrs. McSweeney had told her. Weldon had to ask, "What did they stop you in the street for? One of them looked mad, the other one didn't."

"Oh, they're suppose to stop everybody, but kids and old women."

"Okay, Janice, you may as well unsaddle your horse and let her rest. We'll do the same. We still have over an hour to wait."

Darkness had brought the lamp lighter out on the hotel porch. Janice and Butch were standing at the corner. As the globe was lifted, and the wick raised, Butch whispered loud, "Don't turn around, and don't be stupid enough to raise your hands. Where are all them fellers situated, and how many of them are healthy enough to use a gun?"

"If by situated, you mean where are they, they're at the two back tables. That would be just to the right of the back door. If you are about to start shooting, I'd be obliged if I could tell the bartender first. He's my brother."

"You've got five minutes, and don't make any fast moves. Two more of us are coming in the back door, and will shoot at fast moving men."

The Bartender and his brother were standing at the front of the bar, as Butch and Janice casually walked in and ordered a drink. The men at the tables started to get up, but the one who talked like a boss, shook his head no.

They returned to their card game, with one or two of them lifting their eyes toward Janice and Butch, every couple of minutes. Butch watched the clock, and bumped Janice on the arm. "Get ready, and watch the back door. When you see that latch start to rise, hit the floor with your gun out."

The latch lifted, and before Shorty and Weldon could rush in with guns drawn, Janice had pulled hers, and ran the thirty feet to the table. Men scooted back their chairs, trying to grab for their guns. Janice had hers stuck in the back of the bosses head. "You get a gun out, and this fat man is dead! Shuck 'em!" She motioned with her eyes and head, not her gun.

Shorty and Weldon started taking guns as Butch walked up. "Shorty, she's crazy! I told her to hit the floor! But did she? Nooo, she had to jump over here and take a chance of getting her brains blowed out!" He turned to Janice. "What in the hell do you think would have happened if you'd picked the wrong man to stick that gun at?"

"With all that brass, no chance."

The fat Spaniard started talking fast. "Señors, do you not know who I am? I am Lieutenant Fernando Argus! Lieutenant for Lieutenant Governor Edwardo Luna! I have been sent here to up hold the law. As you have none.

Shorty wanted to reach over and slap his head into the next county. "Argus, the la..." he was cut off.

"That is Lieutenant Argus, to you, Señor! Remember that, and you just might live. If that is my wish. And right now, that is not my wish. I think I will have you shot!"

"Feller, it ain't what you wish! That kid with the gun buried at the back of your head is waiting for me to shake mine up and down. Your brains, if you got any, would be blowed plumb to Texas. Now shut the hell up, and get to your feet! You and your boys are going to replace Sheriff Garrett in his jail."

"Señor! If you release a prisoner of the Territory, you will be shot!"

"Remind me of that after you're locked up, ass hole! Lets go, and if your boys over there start shooting, guess who gets it first. So, if I were you, when we get into ear shot, I'd start screaming my head off."

And he did start yelling, "Ramon, Lupe, it is me, your Commander! Do not shoot! We are prisoners, put down your guns, and open the door!"

Janice patted him on the shoulder. "That sure was the smart way to do that. I thought for sure I'd get to blow your brains out." She laughed.

While Shorty was getting Pat from the cell, Weldon was holding the other men, ready to push them into the same hole. Butch moved beside an old friend, and started talking low. "Mel, what in the hell's going on? Why'd you tie up with turd bags like this? I'd bet it was money, right?"

"Yeah, we get paid more ever week than we made in a month with Sam. What are you doing now? You're not the law, are you?"

"Naw, me and Weldon are just helping this kid out. Sam and his brothers killed his folks, and left him a good-sized ranch down in the Rio Hondo Valley. I guess you know, after talking with Jess and Otis, Sam's dead."

Mel got real serious. "Yeah, yeah, they told me about Sam an' Ed, an' Nick. But what's the name of this kid's ranch? Wouldn't happen to be the Whip Cord, would it?" He was looking Butch in the eyes.

Pat called out, "Okay, Mel, its lock up time."

Butch held up his hand to Pat. Just a minute Pat, Mel is about to tell me something. Ain't you Mel, and it is the Whip Cord Ranch."

"Yeah, sure thing. Argus give that ranch to Jess and Otis for telling him about a U. S. Marshal heading this way. Oh, and so you'll know, Butch, when I saw it was you and Weldon along, I didn't shoot at none of y'all."

"Thanks, Mel. I'll do what I can for you. Maybe not much, but some."

Mel was herded into the cell with the other men. Argus was hollering for a lawyer. He was told he would get one in Santa Fe, so he shut his mouth.

Pat walked from one to the other, shaking their hands. "Shorty, I don't know but what I'd be dead before this time tomorrow, if not for y'all four. Weldon, Butch, you've got my forever thanks, and if ever I can do anything, come by or send for me. I'll be there. And now, Jack. You're..."

Before he said another word, Shorty, Weldon and Butch started laughing. Janice stuck out her hand to Pat, as he looked to each man. Slowly he took her hand, thinking she was Jack. "Janice McCord, at your service, Sir." She smiled right big. It started soaking in, Pat knew something was strange. He jerked his hand away, with his eyes bugged out.

"Janice McCord! Did you say, Janice McCord? You mean to tell me it was Janice who out gunned the Bristol gang at the McCord Ranch! You mean to tell me it was you that out gunned Ed Kraymon!! Come on now, enough!"

"Yep, its me, Janice. I just had to become Jack while I got the Kraymons for killing my folks. But from now on, I'm Janice again."

Butch stepped in, "Hold on a minute, Jack, I've got something to tell you about your ranch. Mel just told me that Argus gave it to Jess and Otis."

"He what? Why that loony sack of horse hockey! I'll..." She jerked her gun and headed for the cell-block. Shorty grabbed her.

"Let me go, Shorty! I'll kill that son- of- a-she-goat right now!"

"Hold it Janice! We'll let the law do that. Pat will get a good-sized posse and run these boys to Santa Fe, where Governor Wallace will handle 'em. He can even send word to Fort Stanton. Maybe the cavalry will want to be in on this, just in case the Lieutenant Governor is trying to overthrow the Territory. To beat that, we've still got to get Jess and Otis off of your ranch."

"My God! You're right, lets ride!"

"Not tonight. We'll pull out at daylight. Now lets all get some sleep."

Janice worried all night and got very little sleep. It was just pink in the east when she knocked on Shorty's door. "Shorty, can we go now. I've got this really awful bad feeling that we ought'a be there."

With everyone up, they ate a fast breakfast and hit the road to the ranch. Topping the north rim of the Rio Hondo Valley, they saw a large column of smoke curling high in the windless sky. Tears welled in Janice's eyes. "We're too late! They've gone and done it! They're a couple of low life tubs of rotten sheep dip! You just wait until I get them in my sights again. They're dead! I should have killed them back on that ridge!"

She kicked her horse off the hill at a dangerous pace. When she hit lower ground, her horse was in an all out run. Shorty, Weldon and Butch were yards behind, staying away from the flying clods from her horses' hooves.

Shorty pulled beside her. "Janice, slow down! You'll ride on to them."

"Boy, I sure hope so! I'm going..." Shots were heard loud and clear. First pistol shots echoed from the barn, and then a loud boom from the house.

Shorty reached and took the reins of Janice's horse. "Hold on Janice! You ain't going to barge in there and get your head blowed off. Now slow down before I pull you off that horse. Let's see what's going on first. That looks like a haystack that's on fire. No smoke is coming from the house or barns. Jim must have seen them coming and made it to the house and a gun."

Janice swung her horse wide. "Come on! We'll come in from the river side. We'll have a clear view of the house and barns, but still have plenty of cover for us in the trees. We won't be seen."

They dismounted a hundred and fifty yards below the barn. From there they could see Otis and Jess fire a couple of shots toward the house, then duck back out of sight. Jim was crouched behind the porch and would fire a shot that ripped boards from the barn door. Janice laughed out loud. "He's got daddy's fifty caliber Spencer! There ain't enough wood in that barn to stop just one of those slugs. Hay's the only thing in there to hide behind."

When Jess took aim for another shot, Janice brought her rifle to her shoulder. She took a careful, straight aim at the side of his head, then lowered it to his gun arm. Jess' gun went flying and he hit the ground, screaming his head off. Otis reached to pull him back inside, when Shorty's bullet took him high in the shoulder. Both men were down.

As they walked toward the barn, Jim advanced toward Otis and Jess with the Spencer. Weldon reached over and patted Janice on the shoulder. "You could have taken Jess' head off with that shot. What made you not do it?"

"Y'all probably think I've went and gone soft, but that's not it. He wouldn't have known where it came from, or who done it. I want them to know I'm the reason they'll both hang. My testimony in court will close this case for good, and end their worthless lives. It's a shame, everything they've done."

Jim was standing with the Spencer in his hands. "Boy, am I ever glad to see y'all. They've been shooting at me since sunup. I'd just got to the barn to start the chores, when I seen 'em coming. I high tailed it for this sharps and was going to come upon the barn from behind. They saw me leave the house and started shooting. They couldn't leave the barn, and I couldn't get back in the house or make a run for the woods.

"Jack, I'm sorry I doubted you and caused you so much trouble. If you want to fire me, I'll understand. I couldn't blame you one bit."

"No, I'm not going to fire you, but from now on, you can call me Janice. I'm alive again." There was that pretty, little crooked smile.

"Janice! You mean you're a her?" Jim's knees started to buckle.

Butch put his arm around her shoulders. "And a damn pretty her, too. Don't you think?" He stared at Jim, who was looking for a place to sit down.

Otis and Jess had their wounds taken care of, and were tied to their saddles for the trip into Lincoln. Otis was the most upset. "A God damned pussy faced girl with nine lives, is what brought down the whole Kraymon and Bristol gangs! Bull shit! I still don't believe it! It's a damn trick of some kind!"

Janice got right in his face. "Your stupid brother was who brought both gangs down! When Sam and all of your brothers raped my mother, and killed my family, that's what brought all of you down! I would have hunted you all over hell if I'd had to! I made the promise that I'd see all of you dead by my gun. Maybe I won't be pulling the trigger on you two, but it was my gun that caused you to be caught. I'll at least get to see you hang, turd bag! There is nobody still alive as sorry as you two!"

Shorty reached over and shook hands with Janice. "Janice, you know where to get hold of me if ever there's a need. Pat Garrett will be in touch with you, so you can testify against these two. What are you going to do with the ranch? Run it, or sell out?"

"I'll never sell Whip Cord. But it would make it a lot easier for me, if Weldon and Butch will stay and work. Weldon can be my ramrod and hire all the help we'll need, and by Butch staying on, he could stay out of trouble with the law. What do you say, fellers? Can we make a deal?"

Weldon nodded to Butch. Butch laughed, saying, "If you're as good a boss as you are partner to ride the trail with, I'd say it's a deal. To beat that, maybe between the both of us, we can keep you home and out of trouble."

Janice smiled. "Don't bet on it. I kind'a like that sort'a life. So Shorty, if you ever need a dad-gumed good deputy, I'd like to be it. I think I could get use to killing dirt bags like these two."